RUIN

a ruin novel

#1 *New York Times* Bestselling Author

RACHEL VAN DYKEN

Ruin
A Ruin Novel
by Rachel Van Dyken

Copyright © 2013 RACHEL VAN DYKEN

RUIN
Copyright © 2013 RACHEL VAN DYKEN
ISBN: 978-1-946061-68-3
Cover Design by Jill Sava, Love Affair With Fiction
Formatting by Jill Sava, Love Affair With Fiction

RUIN

AUTHOR NOTE

When I originally wrote this story a few years ago, I did it with one purpose in mind. Finish it before my uncle lost his battle with cancer. My publisher at the time was kind enough to let me out of my non-compete so I could publish this book in his honor. The first two weeks of sales went toward paying his medical bills.

Cancer is... well it is, isn't it? It's this huge, giant, horrible thing. It exists to torture us, to force us to cower in fear. While watching my uncle battle cancer, the one thing I was always in amazement over was his lack of fear. It's like he KNEW it was going to be okay, even though the end was near, he KNEW without a shadow of a doubt where he was going, and he was at peace with it. Writing this book was my therapy; it was my way of dealing with something horrible, my way of paying tribute to him.

Ruin also would not have been possible had I not been

introduced to Joyce Meyer. I remember reading one of her books (The Confident Woman), and she started talking about fear, about doing it afraid. The phrase has stuck with me for LIFE. I swear I still think about it on a daily basis, so thanks to Joyce Meyer's wisdom and incredibleness, I wanted to add that phrase into this book so that it would continue to help people who are maybe struggling with conquering their fears. Do it afraid is one of Joyce Meyer's mantras, and now it's one of mine; hopefully, after finishing this book, it will be yours too.

Ruin is sexy, it's still funny (I can't do straight-up angst! Not even if I tried!), and it's heartwarming. You may cry, but I promise you'll be smiling through your tears!

To all of you who have been impacted by cancer, this book is for you, and to Uncle Jobob, who eight weeks after this book was originally published, lost his battle with liver cancer, thank you for being such a wonderful example of what strength is.

Laugh in the face of what makes you afraid.

Do it, even when fear threatens to hold you back, keep walking anyway, conquer it—afraid.

Hugs, RVD

PROLOGUE

"**C**an you hear me? Kiersten?" His voice was so close; maybe if I closed my eyes it would feel more real. I reached up to touch him, but all I could feel was air. He wasn't there. He was gone.

So it really happened.

I blinked a few times and tried to focus on what was in front of me. It looked like him, but he was standing too far away. Why was I lying on the ground?

"Come back to me." *His mouth moved as he spoke softly.* "Not like this, Kiersten. Not like this, baby." *His light blue eyes flared with need.* "Everything is going to be just fine. I promise."

But it wasn't fine. I knew it. He knew it.

He was gone — and I was hallucinating.

I'd lost the love of my life — my best friend. How many times could people experience loss before they died too? Before heartache consumed them? Memories flooded my brain, memories of my parents, memories of him playing football, memories of all the notes he gave me.

Our first kiss.

Our final time together.

And then, the hospital.

We hadn't been given enough time — and I hated God for taking everyone from me. I hated that in the end, I would always be alone to mourn the loss of those I loved.

I reached for his face one last time. This time my fingers came into contact with warm skin. It was all a dream. Well, if it was a dream, I was going to enjoy the way his smile lit up the room. His lips touched my forehead. I closed my eyes and prayed for God to take me too.

Because I knew the moment I woke up, I'd have to say goodbye all over again, and this time I wasn't sure I'd ever heal from the experience of that one word leaving my lips. Goodbye — whoever invented that word should burn in Hell.

ONE

Weakness is just pain leaving the body.

Kiersten

I repeated the same mantra over and over again until I thought I was going to lose my mind. It wasn't real. I was having the nightmare again. It wasn't real.

Never a good sign when you wake yourself up because you're screaming so loud. Footsteps neared the door, and then it burst open, revealing my roommate, you know, the one I just met a few hours ago.

"Are you okay?" She took a tentative step through the door and crossed her arms. "I heard screaming."

Right. I was a freak. I wanted a fresh start, and what did I get? A gold star for traumatizing my roommate, the only friendly face I'd met since arriving at the University of Washington.

"Um, yeah." I managed to keep my voice from shaking. "I know it's weird, but I still have night terrors." At the look of disbelief on her face, I added quickly, "But only when I'm really stressed out." *And when I'm on heavy medication,* but I left that part out.

"Oh." She licked her lips and looked back out into the hallway. "Do you want me to sleep on the floor or something? I mean, I will if you're scared."

Bless her southern hospitality-filled heart. "No." I smiled. "I'm good. I hope I didn't scare you."

"Yeah, well…" Lisa waved me off. "I didn't really like that lamp in my room anyway."

"My screaming broke a lamp?" I cringed.

"No." She shook her head. "My fall broke the lamp. Seems jumping out of your bunk bed at one in the morning's a contact sport. My lamp being the main target. No worries." She sighed. "It didn't suffer. It shattered on contact with the floor. And then again after I slipped on the teddy bear that also fell. And that's great since it broke my fall onto the floor, making it so I escaped with two faint bruises."

I covered my face with my hands. "Holy crap! I'm so sorry!"

"Nah, it's fine. I'm a walking accident." She laughed. "But if you plan on screaming all night, I'm taking the floor. My lamp killing days are behind me."

Smiling, I nodded. "Sure. I just… I don't want you to—"

"Stop apologizing." Lisa's smile was warm and inviting. "Oh, and I sleepwalk, so if you wake up to me standing over you, try not to punch me in the face."

"Wow, we're sure a fun pair."

She grabbed a blanket from my bed and threw it onto the floor. "You know those little comment sections in the housing part of registration?"

"Yeah?"

"I swear it's a setup to put all of us weirdos together."

I yawned.

"I need a pillow," Lisa announced. "I'll be right back. No more screaming. Close your eyes, and in the morning we'll go boy-hunting. Dream about that."

"Boys?"

"Uh…" Lisa tucked her brown hair behind her ear. "That is, unless you're interested in girls. I mean, that's cool if you bat for the other team; I was just sayin'—"

"No, no, no." A weak laugh squeezed past my lips. Did I *look* like I batted for the other team? "No, nothing like that. I've just never had a boyfriend."

"You poor soul!" Was she serious? "How did you survive?"

"Netflix, Johnny Depp, books. I powered through." I shrugged. "Trust me, if you grew up in the town I did, you wouldn't have dated either."

"Oh yeah? Why?" She held up her hand really quick and ran out of the room. When she came back, she had her pillow in hand. Throwing it onto the floor, she sat with her legs crossed and yawned. "Okay, you may continue."

"Guys…" I lay on my left side so I could fully face her. "I didn't date them because my town was so dang small that if I even sneezed in the wrong direction, my mom said *bless you* before I even got it out. I mean, the one time I got a bad grade on my report card, it made the newspaper."

"Huh? What the hell kind of town does that?"

"One that literally documents how many people visit it during the high season."

"High season?" Lisa asked.

"Tourist season. When people go wine-tasting. Last year we had five hundred, which is more people than our entire town put together."

"This information makes me depressed," Lisa announced. "So no cute boys then?"

"Mayor's son was cute."

"Oh, that's cool!" she gushed.

"Yup, the quarterback of the football team thought so too."

"Did that one make the news?" She cringed.

I wrinkled my nose and nodded. "It did. Along with my bad grade."

"I would have taken the bad grade."

"Agreed." I laughed. It felt good that someone could empathize with how bad it royally sucked to be the center of attention. Tension slowly left my body.

"Well, we'll have to rectify this situation immediately." She licked her lips. "I know plenty of guys. I met at least ten at orientation this morning. One of them had tattoos." She sighed longingly. "I'm a sucker for tattoos."

"But they cover your skin." I pointed out. "And a tattoo is forever. I mean, don't you think it's kind of trashy?"

"Who are you?" She squinted. "Apparently, your small town was built underneath a rock."

"Um…" I laughed. "My point exactly."

"Trust me, the only reason you don't like tattoos is because you've never seen them spread over a hot body. You'll change real fast when you see that yummy goodness on a six-pack. Hell, last time I saw a shirtless guy with tattoos, I asked if I could lick him."

"What did he say?"

Lisa sighed. "Yes…" Then she shrugged. "We dated for a week, then I left him for greener pastures."

"Bigger tattoo?"

"How'd you know!" She threw her head back and laughed.

"I was kind of known for being the school slut, but it was better than not being known at all."

I wasn't sure how I felt about that, but I kept my mouth shut, especially considering I'd never even kissed a guy before. Too embarrassed to admit my inexperience, I just shrugged. "Well, that's what college is for. It's a fresh start, right?"

"Right." Her eyes flickered away from mine for a brief moment. Her smile fell from her face. "Well, at any rate, we should get some sleep if we're going boy-hunting tomorrow."

"Right." I yawned again. "And thanks, Lisa, for checking on me."

"What type of roommate would I be if I didn't come running?"

"One who didn't kill lamps and wake up with two bruises?"

"Damn lamp," she muttered. "Night, Kiersten."

"Night."

TWO

If it looks like a rat, smells like a rat, and talks like a rat, it's probably a freaking rat.

Kiersten

"**N**ame?" The guy at Registration didn't look up, merely paused as his fingers hovered over the iPad. I'd woken up at seven so I could make early registration at eight. Tables were lined outside the Student Center in prison-like fashion. At least twenty upperclassmen stood in front of the tables with packets and bored expressions.

"Kiersten," I answered.

He let out an irritated sigh. "There are over thirty-five thousand students on this campus, and you want me to look you up by your first name, Kiersten?"

"Sorry. Uh… Rowe. Kiersten Rowe."

He typed away. "Well, Rowe Kiersten Rowe, it looks like you're registered for nineteen credits and have yet to decide on a major."

What was he? A profiler? "That's right." I leaned back on

my heels and cleared my throat. He still didn't look up.

"Hmm…" His hands moved fluidly over the screen. "All right, I'm sending your schedule to your school email." He set the iPad down and grabbed a packet. "Campus map, mailbox number, student email, everything you need is in this package. If you have any questions, you can ask your RA."

I hoped he meant resident advisor because if he meant something else, I had no idea what he was talking about.

"Okay." I took the packet he thrust in my face. "What about my student ID card?"

"Next!" He lifted his head and shot me another irritated glance.

"Excuse me." I stood my ground. "Where do I get my student ID card?"

His shoulders slumped. "Look, Kiersten, I have a line of a few hundred students; I said everything you need to know is in your packet, so look in your packet. If you have questions, ask your RA. We…" He pointed at himself then at her. "… are finished here."

What the hell was his problem?

I wasn't sure if I was embarrassed or just irritated. Cursing, I held the packet to my chest and stomped off. I turned around to send him one last seething glare and ran smack dab into a tree.

Or at least it felt like a tree.

But trees weren't warm.

And they didn't have one, two, three, four, six, Good Lord, eight? Eight-packs? Furthermore, had I actually been feeling said person's eight-pack? And, dear God, I was counting. I had touched each muscle. And great, my hand was still firmly placed against the guy's stomach.

I jerked my hand back and closed my eyes.

"Were you just counting my abs?" His voice sounded amused. It also sounded like a movie star voice, the type that makes you want to jump into the TV screen. It was deep, strong, and had a slight accent I couldn't place. British? Scottish?

I took my lower lip between my teeth and thought about what to say. Well, there really was no way out of it. I nodded. "Sorry, I just…" I shouldn't have looked. If I could go back in time, I would have. I had no idea that one look would devastate me. Weeks from now I would regret that one look, for one reason and one reason only.

His eyes held my ruin.

"Weston." He held out his hand. "And you are?"

Screwed. "Kiersten." I clutched the packet tighter against my chest. He squinted at my hands then looked at his.

"You have a germ thing?"

"Huh? What? No?"

"You have a disease?" His hand was still between us; it was getting more awkward by the minute. *Just put it away!*

"Um, no."

"Good." He moved his hand from safe territory, and suddenly he was touching me, well, touching my packet, but I could have sworn I felt every bit of his heat as he slowly peeled it from my grip and freed up my hands. "Now," he held out his hand again, "where were we?"

What the heck was wrong with me? It wasn't that I didn't want to shake his hand. It was just that I was embarrassed, and I wanted to leave, and I wasn't sure if he was just being nice to me to be nice or — wow, I needed therapy.

Clearing my throat, I reached over and shook his hand. At his smirk, I panicked. He clenched my hand within his and

RACHEL VAN DYKEN

looked down at our joining, then mumbled something under his breath. I felt the loss when he finally released my fingers.

"See?" He handed back my packet. "That wasn't so hard, now was it?"

"No." I swallowed, and my eyes darted across the crowded lawn. I seriously couldn't stare at him in the face; that was how gorgeous he was. I'd never seen such a good-looking guy in real life before. Sure, I'd seen them in magazines and movies, but this guy... He was living, breathing, walking sex. And considering I had no experience in that department, I was putting up every wall I could think of in order to remember to breathe.

His eyes were a pale blue, his hair a golden blond that was a little too long and curled by his ears. And his smile. Well, his smile would probably haunt me for the rest of my life. It was easy, and his dimples only made it worse. And then there was his smell. A mixture of some sort of cinnamon and something else I couldn't really put my finger on. It irritated me how easy it seemed for him to smile as if nothing was wrong in the world when everything felt like it inside. He wanted to shake my hand and know my name, and I wanted to get the hell out of there and sit in my room, preferably rocking back and forth in a corner until my anti-depressants decided to kick into high gear.

"So," he said with a chuckle. "We go from you touching my abs, straight to insulting me by not shaking my hand, and then to daydreaming. That sound about right?"

"Oh my gosh." I closed my eyes. "I'm sorry. It's my first day, and I'm just... nervous." There, that sounded good, not at all like I was seconds away from having a minor freak out.

"Let me help?"

"But I don't know you," I blurted.

"Sure you do." Somehow he maneuvered himself around me so that his arm was resting on my shoulder, and we were walking back toward my dorm. Holy crap. This is how girls were taken advantage of. Panicking, I searched the lawn for Lisa, but she was nowhere to be found.

"No." I dug my heels into the ground. "I, uh, I need to find my roommate and my ID card! I have to grab my ID card. Well, first I need to find my RA…" I sounded like a lost kid at the park. Funny, because most of the time I felt that way, lost, like a missing puzzle piece that forgot it was a part of the rest of the puzzle. The outcast, the loner the—

"—I believe," he said, smirking, "that I said I'd help you."

"I don't need that kind of help," I whispered.

"Huh?" He stopped walking and then burst out laughing. "Holy shit, I think I may love you."

Heart meet stomach.

He kept laughing and pulled me tighter to him. Well, at least my uncle wouldn't have to worry about paying for college. I was like ten minutes away from being taken. Like in the movie, *Taken*, only I didn't have a badass dad to come save me. My heart clenched again.

"I'm not going to take advantage of you," Weston said. "No offense, but you look way too innocent for my tastes, which you again proved when you wrongfully assumed I wanted to help myself into your pants."

My face erupted in flames.

"Also…" We kept walking. "You're a freshman. I don't do freshmen, as in, I don't date them. Hell, I don't usually even help them, but you did almost knock me over, and regardless of how much you deny it, you were counting my abs—"

"I wasn't—"

"You were." He sighed wistfully. "I watched your mouth move, one, two, three. It's eight, by the way, an eight-pack. I work out a lot."

"Great," I said through clenched teeth.

"Aw, Lamb, don't be embarrassed." He stopped and released me.

"Lamb?"

"Pure." He smiled. "And lost." Shrugging, he pointed to my dorm. "Like a little lamb."

"Well, thanks for the walk back to my dorm." I brushed past him, but he grabbed my wrist.

"Don't you want to talk to the RA about the ID card?"

"Yeah, I'm going to go get her right now." I jerked free. "So, thanks for… everything." I was redefining the meaning of socially awkward.

He licked his full lips and smiled again. "Okay, you go ask her."

"Okay." I stumbled backward, almost tripping on my own feet, and made my way up the stairs to the dorm.

Once inside, I could feel him still staring at me.

I turned around.

He was grinning.

I waved.

He waved back.

Seriously? What kind of sick game was this?

Muttering a curse, I read through the different floors and located the RA's room. Sixth floor. Of course. I went to the stairs and slowly made my way up.

By the time I reached the sixth floor, I was ready to forgo the entire ID card in favor of a nap. One of the side effects of my medicine. Sometimes they made me sleepy. Other times I had such vivid dreams it was like starring in Alice in Wonderland

With a groan, I forced my feet to take me to the end of the hall. Room 666. That had to be a joke, right? I knocked twice on the door.

It swung open, revealing my tree… "Weston?"

"Lamb." He opened his door wider. "How can I *help* you?"

THREE

I should have left well enough alone.

Kiersten

took a few steps back to examine the number next to the door. "I, uh… is the RA not here? Did you break into her room?"

"One…" He held up his finger. "I'm a bit insulted that you think I'd have to break into a girl's room to get in. Believe me. I knock, they open, I walk in. It's as simple as that."

I bet it was.

"Two…" He held up two fingers. "You're looking at the RA. Now, why don't you come in, and I'll explain to you how the whole student ID card thing works."

Pressing my lips together, I gave him a firm nod and walked into the room. It was clean. Not what I expected from what I'd read about guys and hygiene.

"So…" Weston walked over to his bed and sat. "Let me see your schedule, and I'll answer whatever questions you have."

I was still processing the fact that he was my RA. "I don't get it. I could have sworn the Freshman RA was a female."

"Sex change," Weston said with a straight face. "I was a confused child."

"Funny." I rolled my eyes. "Seriously? I requested an all-girls dorm and got put in a co-ed building, and then my RA is a—" I was going to say hot guy but refrained from embarrassing myself.

"Sex god." He said it for me. "I know some people have all the luck." With a heavy sigh, he pulled a chunk of papers from my packet and whistled. "Looks like you've got a hell of a schedule. Nineteen credits? No major? You don't seem like the indecisive type."

I wanted to tell him he didn't know me. In fact, I wanted to snap at him. What did he know of my life? My past? My reasons for not committing? As if sensing my anger, my cell went off; I looked at the screen. Uncle JoBob. I called him Jo. He'd been taking care of me for the past two years. Ever since… everything happened.

I pressed ignore. Uncle Jo would flip if he heard a male voice in the background, and Weston didn't seem the quiet type to me. No, he was a flaunter. Crap, he even looked like he was flexing sitting there, though I couldn't be sure. He had a long-sleeved white shirt on with ripped jeans.

"So…" He pulled out a pen and scribbled something on the paper. "The campus map is going to be your bread and butter. Don't get lost, and don't walk by yourself at night, okay?"

"I think I can handle it." I snatched the paper from him. "ID card?"

"Right." He stood and shoved his hands in his pockets. "I

circled the building on the map. Smile bright for your picture, Lamb."

I grimaced, "Are you going to call me that all year?"

"Would you rather I call you something else?" he whispered, his lips close enough to touch mine.

"Um, no thanks." My voice shook.

"You sure about that?" He stared at my lips. I took a step back, he took another step forward.

"I thought you weren't into freshmen." I was backed into a corner, literally. I felt something sharp against my back.

"Maybe I'm changing my mind," he offered, tilting my chin toward his face. "I always was a sucker for redheads."

My eyes narrowed. "Strawberry blonde."

"Redhead."

"Light red."

He sighed. "Hate to break it to you, but your hair is red. You're a redhead, not a light redhead, not a strawberry-blonde. Accept it, embrace it, love it. Because you're freaking gorgeous."

Okay, so that was forward. I licked my lips and mumbled a thanks before ducking away from him and making a beeline toward the door.

"Forgetting something?" his voice came from behind me.

"No?" I froze.

His hands were on my shoulders. Slowly, he turned me to face him and handed the map and my packet to me. "There you go. Remember what I said, no walking alone at night and smile wide."

"I'll try."

"Don't try." His grip tightened on the packet. "Be smart. Walk in pairs. Use the buddy system. Don't drink things that smell funny—"

"And don't go into guy's rooms alone, even if he is an RA."

His smile fell. "Touché."

I jerked my packet free from his hands and walked out.

"Use the elevator!" he called after me.

So that was how he did it. Bastard. I looked up. Sure enough, there was a sign that pointed to the elevator. I went to press the down button and refused to look back, even though I knew his door was open, and he was still staring at me.

FOUR

Embarrass myself in front of the hottest guy on the planet? Check.

Kiersten

"**W**here were you?" Lisa sounded outraged at my absence as she threw up her hands in surrender. "I looked everywhere! And Gabe couldn't find you either!"

"Gabe?" I walked into the room.

Lisa pointed to the couch. "Gabe."

"I'm Gabe." A guy with dark hair that fell to his chin lifted his hand into the air in a wave. He had a nose ring and so many tattoos lining his arms that I thought I was going to have a seizure from all the moving parts.

"Hey." I waved back. "Nice to meet you. And how was Gabe looking for me if he doesn't know who I am?"

"Facebook." Lisa shrugged. "I stalked you, pulled up your picture, pushed it into his face, and I—"

"Yelled," Gabe interrupted. "She yelled. A bit of an

exaggerator that one. She had it in her mind that you got kidnapped."

"Sort of did," I grumbled.

"What!" Lisa shrieked.

"Are you on drugs?" I leaned in to examine her eyes.

"Coffee," Gabe offered. "She's had enough to kill a person."

"Who took you!" Lisa grabbed my arms.

"Me," a voice said from the door. Aw crap, did he have a tracking device on me or something?

Lisa's mouth dropped open. It looked like she was going to pass out. Even Gabe looked stunned. Okay, right, Weston was hot, but not hot enough to render both sexes speechless.

I turned on my heel. "What do you want?"

"Ooh, touchy. I like." He gave a sloppy grin. "You left your purse." He handed me my black Dooney and Burke. "I didn't look through it, just so you know."

Well, I hadn't even thought about that possibility. My pills were in there. He'd probably label me a freak if he saw them. What kind of person needed meds to deal with her life? I did. I just wish I didn't have to take them.

"Uh, thanks." I tried dismissing him. Instead, he looked around the room, his eyes seeming to focus on every single detail from the paint to the carpet, and then finally, he stepped back out into the hallway. "Oh!" He held up his hand. "I almost forgot."

Weston pulled a sharpie from his pocket and snatched my hand before I was able to put it back into my pocket. With swift movements, he wrote a phone number onto my palm and blew across it until it dried.

I felt that breeze all the way down to my toes. I think I may have swayed on my feet too, but I couldn't be certain because I blacked out for a few seconds.

"There." He lifted his head and looked into my eyes. "Just in case the lamb can't find her way home."

"Cute."

"Thank you." He winked and walked out the door.

The room fell silent. I shrugged and turned to face Lisa. Her mouth was open, and she looked alive, but nothing was coming out of her except for a slight moan. Was she having a stroke?

Gabe jumped up from the couch and went to slam the door closed

"Shit!" Gabe clapped his hands and swore again. "Outside of football games, I've never seen him. I mean, he doesn't talk to people. He never leaves his entourage!"

"Entourage?" The only experience I'd had with that particular word was watching the show on my computer. Did that mean he had lots of people around him all the time? Weird, because when I was with him, he was alone. "He's our RA."

"SHUT UP!" Lisa looked faint. "Oh, I need to sit, I need to sit. Gabe bring a fan; I think I'm going to pass out."

Gabe rolled his eyes. "Good to know how I compare to the god."

"You aren't even in the same atmosphere as Weston Michels."

Michels? Why did that last name sound familiar?

"Thanks, cousin."

"Anytime."

"Cousin?" I asked.

"Oh right, Gabe's my cousin." She waved me off and started doing breathing exercises.

Well, at least she wasn't already bringing strange men back to our room. Gabe took a seat next to her, his grin wide.

"Okay, what am I missing?" I sat on the couch and leaned forward. "Is this Weston guy important?"

Gabe let out a laugh and then slapped his leg. "You're shitting me, right? Where have you been living?"

"Bickelton."

"Huh?" He leaned in as if to examine me. I was speaking English, right?

"Small town." Lisa smacked him and then focused on me again. "I can't believe you don't know who Weston is. Seriously? You said you watched TV."

"I do," I defended myself. "Well, I mean, I watch Netflix, and I read magazines and stuff, you know, when they're available at our corner store."

"Holy shit, you live in the fifties." Gabe snorted.

I glared.

"Weston Michels." Lisa typed the name into her phone and then handed it to me.

I should have known.

He had an IMDb website. Not a good sign. That screamed entertainment industry. I scrolled further down.

And there it was.

The Forbes article had been done around two years before, about the same time as the accident. I hadn't been much of a social butterfly then. In fact, I distinctly remember Uncle Jo threatening to throw me out if I didn't leave my room.

I tapped the screen, making the image bigger. His hair was longer now. He looked happier, easy even, in the Forbes picture. I swallowed the dryness in my throat as I continued reading and looked at the next picture, Weston Michels and his dad, Randy Michels, one of the richest men in the world. They moved to the states when Weston was eight, explaining his accent, I knew he sounded British!

"He's like a hybrid," Gabe said, pulling the phone from my grip. "Weston Michels is like two months away from inheriting a multi-billion-dollar fortune."

"Why is he our RA then?" I wondered aloud.

"Punishment for his many sins." Gabe exhaled. "And when you're Randy Michel's son, you don't sin in silence. The whole damn world sees you for what you are."

"What you are?" I repeated. "What did he do?"

"Raped a girl," Gabe said. "At least that's the rumor. His family paid her off. They were dating at the time. She dumped him, then he forced himself on her or something like that. Details are a bit fuzzy." Gabe yawned. "Rumor had it that he was going to drop out of school, but his dad must have made him own up to everything."

"So…" I wrung my hands together, trying to understand. "Our RA is an alleged rapist? How is that okay with the university?"

"How, indeed?" Lisa finally spoke up, "The man's a god. I bet the bitch set him up. No way would that guy risk that much."

"But rich guys tend to be controlling," I said, stomach dropping as I remembered the exchange Weston and I had had in his dorm room. Holy crap, was I almost taken advantage of? I wrapped my sweater tighter around my chest.

"Just goes to show money buys everything." Gabe stretched out on the couch. "He's our RA, didn't get kicked off the football team, and rumor has it just spent the weekend partying in Malibu. I'd say he's just fine."

"What about the girl?" I asked.

"Ah, Lorelei. She's just fine. The day after the incident, she was seen making out with some other guy, so, yeah, the whole rape thing? Probably not true, though I'd still carry a whistle."

"Whistle?" I repeated. "Like a rape whistle?"

"No." Gabe shook his head. "Like one you use at a basketball game. Are you for real?"

"Yes?"

His gaze examined mine. "I worry about your roommate's safety, Lisa."

"Eh, she's fine."

"Right." Gabe closed his eyes and let out a humorless laugh. "And when the big bad wolf, also known as Weston Michels, decides to pounce on her pasture, what is she gonna do? Hide? Look at her."

Gabe pointed. I stepped back. Lisa tilted her head to the side, her eyes roaming from my outfit to my hair. I shifted uncomfortably and tucked my hair behind my ears.

"We could make her ugly." She thumbed part of my t-shirt and squinted. I swatted her hand away and folded my arms.

"We'd have to shave her head." This from Gabe.

Lisa nodded. "And put a mask over her face."

"It can be done," he agreed.

"Um, no." I stepped back even further. "It can't. And stop worrying about me. I'm fine." Right, as long as I had my medication and at least eight hours of sleep every night, I'd be fine. I clenched my hands, allowing myself to feel that brief pain of my nails digging into my palms. If I could feel pain, that meant I could at least feel, right? Sometimes I needed that little reminder to know I wasn't just a walking zombie.

"All right." Gabe stood. Apparently, the subject was closed. "I'll be back to pick you guys up around nine, okay?"

"Nine?" I asked.

"See ya!" Lisa smacked him on the back as he waltzed out of our room. He was cute, in one of those dark rocker sort of ways, and Lisa was right, I guess. Tattoos weren't so bad. At least on Gabe they weren't bad.

"Stop staring at my cousin," she said, coming up behind me. "He's off-limits, as in, bad news for girls like you. He'd take his one-night stand and kiss you on the cheek in the morning all before you could say no."

"Comforting." I sighed.

"Come on." She gripped my hand. "We've got a lot to do if we're going to have time to get ready for the party tonight. And I still need to get my ID card."

"Yeah, I can help with that," I mumbled softly, briefly remembering Weston's concerned gaze as he told me to take a buddy everywhere with me and be careful. Were rapists that concerned for others' safety? He didn't do it. He couldn't have because he could have easily taken advantage of me, and he didn't. Instead, he helped. Yet the thought lingered… what if?

FIVE

Living is hard — dying is easy. You close your eyes and never open them up again. What's so difficult about that? Nothing really — except it hurts like hell to those you leave behind.

Weston

I should have let well enough alone. My doctor would have told me I was playing with things I should just forget about. After all, he'd say, how much time do you have? I was damn sick of hearing him say that. Ridiculous. Even my dad was tired of the doctors. Then again, I was tired of them when I was eight and was told my mom wasn't going to make it through surgery.

And again, last year, at the hospital when my brother didn't wake up from his... situation. Some people believe our family is cursed. After all, you can't have as much power and money that we do and not suffer the consequences. When I was little, my Sunday School teacher told me that sometimes tragedy happened in order to keep us relying on God.

How much more trusting does God need me to be? I mean, I'd lost everything, and last year almost lost my reputation and football career, all because I said no. Funny, nobody ever talks about guys being taken advantage of.

I gripped the phone in my hands. I had her number. How creepy was I? Seriously. I hacked the school system and pulled her number from it. The poor girl already thought I was stalking her, probably wouldn't help my case if I suddenly called her up and said, "Hey." Loser. I was an absolute loser. I'd never had trouble getting girls; in fact, I felt a bit gun shy after last year.

My entourage helped.

I only called them that because it made it sound so much cooler than it really was. A knock sounded on the door. I got up, but it opened before I had a chance. David strolled in, all three hundred pounds of him, and threw my prescription on the table. "How's it going?"

"Fantastic," I lied and quickly hid the piece of paper I'd written Kiersten's number on.

"You feeling okay?" David leaned forward and pointed the flashlight in my eyes, like some sort of scientist. I slapped it away.

"Fine." I cleared my throat and stood. For a brief moment I felt dizzy; that's what I got for standing up too fast. "Where's James?"

"Out." David sighed as if he was tired of me asking a million questions. "He'll be back to walk you to class. You can walk, right?"

I rolled my eyes. "I can walk. It's not like I'm drunk or anything."

"You stood up too fast," he said to himself, then pulled out his notepad and wrote a few things down. "Have you been feeling dizzy lately? Out of breath?"

Hmm, did meeting a new girl that took my breath away count? How about being dizzy from her perfume? What would David have to say about that?

"My dad pays you to protect me, not nurse me." I scowled.

David's eyes narrowed. "You look pale."

"Shit." I rubbed my face with my hands. "Can I please have one normal moment? Just one, where you aren't scribbling on your damn notepad, and we aren't discussing my father or money or my future or—"

David held up his hand. "Got it. Sorry, Wes."

I felt bad. But at the same time, I was irritated all over again. I'd been on edge for months now, and I knew me snapping at David was just going to be another thing he documented when my father asked for his report.

He glanced around the dorm. "Your room looks nice."

"No small talk." I laughed. "My room looks exactly how it's supposed to, clean and approachable. I am an RA, you know."

"Yes, and I'm the queen," David said dryly.

"Right." I grabbed my keys and phone. "We're going to a party tonight."

"We?" His eyebrows lifted.

"Yes, we. You, James, and myself. I need to meet the rest of the students in my dorm, and I can't do that if I hole up in my room like some sick—" The words died in my throat. I bit down on my lower lip and allowed the dizziness to pass again. "I'm going to go work out."

"Should you be—"

"It's all I have," I snapped again. "I'm not quitting football too, David. Write it down in your little notepad and tell that to my dad. My career is football. I'm too damn good to give it up. The only reason I stayed in college this long was to make everyone happy, but now that—" Again the words faded out. I didn't want to finish the sentence; instead, I shook my head at David.

He seemed to understand. With a jerky nod, he followed me out of the room and into the elevator. I needed to sweat off the stress of the day, but mainly I needed to stop thinking about the girl with the pretty eyes and even prettier hair. It was long, almost to her waist, but so freaking thick that I couldn't stop thinking about what it would feel like to thread my fingers through it.

She was the first girl I'd let touch me since Lorelei. Not that I'd actually let her touch me, more like she plowed into me. Nonetheless, I hadn't flinched. Instead, I'd wanted more.

Clearly, I'd wanted more since I'd all but stalked her for the past few hours. Probably not the way to go about things.

The elevator doors opened with a ding. David and I walked out, and people stared, like *really* stared. You'd think I'd be used to it by now, but I wasn't. I hated it. People always wanted something from me. Funny, because I'd give my left arm to be any one of them. I'd gladly take the place of the guy picking his nose by the front door, or even the chick with glasses and buck teeth. I'd trade spots and run in the opposite direction. Not because I hated my life — nope, it was the exact opposite. I loved life.

The doors to the dorm opened.

A few girls held up cell phones, most likely to take pictures. I sighed. Freshman.

I gave a little wave and continued walking, just as James walked up by David and took my left side.

A few more girls giggled as they crossed paths with me. One appeared to faint.

This was my life.

SIX

*Into the fire — or maybe it's out of the fire and into… wait,
I don't remember. Hell?*

Kiersten

"**Y**ou ready?" Lisa wiped some lip gloss from her mouth and checked herself out in the mirror. "Because I know I am."

I laughed. "Yes, you are." She had on a miniskirt, heels, and a short shirt. I'd never be caught dead wearing something like that. Uncle Jo would kill me. I would want to kill me. I mean, that's how girls got into trouble.

"Okay." She turned, a scowl on her face. "You can't wear that."

"What?" I looked down at my straight-leg jeans and boots; I had a white T-shirt on and my hair in a ponytail.

"It's a party."

"I know." I shrugged. "I'm wearing clothes."

"Yes." Lisa's tone was far from encouraging. "But you're also not a nun, and right now, you look like you're homeschool."

Homeschool? All the kids I knew that were homeschool were completely normal; crap, I'd begged my uncle to homeschool me after everything. I looked down at my clothes and shrugged.

A heavy pounding assaulted the door, and then Gabe burst through. "Damn, cousin, you aiming to get laid tonight?"

She smiled.

Gabe's eyes fell to me. "And you're dressed like a first-grade teacher. Why?"

"Very funny."

"Wasn't kidding." He mock-choked as his eyebrows danced suggestively.

With a sigh, I turned back to Lisa. "This is the type of thing I wear. I don't wear short skirts and belly tops and—"

"See, the very fact that you called this," she pointed at her shirt, "A belly top, tells me one thing."

"What?"

"You need help."

Gabe nodded his agreement.

"Guys, I'm not Cinderella."

Smirking, Gabe leaned in and murmured, "Drop your shoe, I dare you."

"Ohhh, he wants to pick up your shoe." Lisa joked.

"It's a boot," I clarified, lifting my foot to show off the shiny black leather.

"Either or." Gabe gave a flirty shrug. "And clothes or no clothes, you're still hot, but if I were you, and I had Weston–freaking-Michels panting after me, I'd make him work for it."

"I, uh…" Playing with my long ponytail, I looked in the mirror. They were right. I looked Amish. I used to be into fashion, but lately, things just seemed semi-pointless. At least

I was eating and showering — not that Gabe and Lisa needed to know that. It was a giant feat for me to be able to take care of myself.

"Fine." I rolled my eyes. "I'll wear a different shirt, but that's where I draw the line."

Lisa grinned and clapped her hands. "Deal!"

Ten minutes later, and I was really doubting my ability to appear normal. The shirt she'd given me didn't meet the top of my jeans. In fact, there was a good two inches of skin showing. I'd tried to hunch over, but then Gabe started calling me Quasimodo, which made me second-guess the whole humpback look.

The party was being held at the main lobby. Things couldn't get that out of hand, right? I mean, it was a school-sanctioned party. It wasn't as if they'd have drugs and alcohol or anything.

Uncle Jo had warned me about mixing alcohol with my prescription. Apparently, it made people get drunk like twice as fast. Meaning, if I took one drink, I'd be dancing around the lobby with a lampshade on my head. Well, at least I wouldn't be self-conscious about my short shirt anymore.

The minute we walked into the lobby, people stared. It wasn't the type of stare you got when you had food in your teeth, more like a curious stare. Maybe it was Gabe. I stood closer to him, and he wrapped his arms around me and Lisa.

"This happens a lot with Gabe." Lisa laughed and landed a mock punch to his biceps. "People can't figure out if he's hot or just deranged."

"Thanks, Lisa." Gabe's eyes narrowed in her direction, then he whispered in my ear, "But for the record, I'm just hot."

"Of course you are," I said patronizingly.

He threw his head back and laughed. I didn't think I could

ever be attracted to him, but something about him seemed comfortable like if I asked him to drive me the four hours home to Bickelton in the middle of the night, he'd say okay and buy me coffee while he was at it. I'd never really had a friend like that before. It was nice.

"So…" Lisa's gaze scanned the crowd. "Where is he?"

"Your mystery man for the night?" Gabe asked as he walked over to the punch and got us each a cup.

"No." Lisa's eyes continued to dart around the room. "Weston. Where is he? He's the RA, so he has to be here—"

"Do I?" a smooth voice said from behind us. "See, I thought I just had to make an appearance. I didn't think anyone would actually be searching me out."

Other than the music pounding through the sound system, it was quiet. I could tell people were trying to hear what he was saying as they edged toward our little group.

He all but ignored Lisa and Gabe. His eyes focused only on mine. "You came."

"I was forced."

"Coerced." Lisa rolled her eyes.

Gabe watched the exchange with open amusement.

Weston was still staring.

Apparently having enough of the awkwardness, Gabe moved me to the side and held out his hand to Weston. "We think she's homeschool; it's why she doesn't talk." He pointed back to me. I could feel my face heat to five hundred degrees. "But she's cute as hell, so we keep her around. This one is my cousin." He pointed to Lisa. "And I'm pretty sure you and I had a KI class together."

Weston's eyes left mine and landed on Gabe. Nodding, he shook his hand firmly. "Yeah, I think it was archery."

"Best class ever." Gabe sighed.

"Ah, now I remember." Weston laughed. "You're the guy who shot the professor in the ass with the arrow."

"She turned me down." Gabe shrugged.

"Sexual harassment." Lisa fake-coughed.

Waving her off, Gabe continued talking. "How's practice going?"

"He's talking football," Lisa whispered. "Shh, it's like watching a baby turtle trying to find the ocean. He's either going to get eaten because he knows shit about sports, or he's going to swim free into the ocean and discover he's a real boy."

"It's good." Weston ignored us. "You know how practice is, brutal. But it's going to be a good season."

"You think you'll get a bowl this year?" Gabe asked, sounding genuinely interested.

"Good Lord, the turtle made it!" Lisa whispered in my ear.

"Yeah." Weston's eyes flickered to mine before he nodded at Gabe. "Coach is hoping for the championship. After the loss last year to Oregon, we kind of want to redeem ourselves."

"Tell me about it." Gabe sighed. "I hate the Ducks."

"Green and yellow, green and yellow," Lisa sang behind him.

"I will think nothing about punching you in the face if you sing that again," Gabe swore.

Lisa grinned. "Well, my work here is done. I just saw one of the guys I met at registration. He walked in, our eyes met. Now I'm going to meet him in the middle of the dance floor."

When she left, Gabe murmured, "She likes to narrate her own life."

"Cool." I laughed. "She needs her own soundtrack."

"Don't tell her that." Gabe shook his head. "I wouldn't put it past her to start singing rather than talking. And I'm already losing IQ points by hanging out with her."

The conversation slid into a lull. Weston was still staring. Gabe's grin grew wider by the minute. Finally, he mumbled something about spiking the punch and walked off. Which really just meant that Weston was the worst RA in the history of RA's. Especially if he was okay with Gabe spiking things.

"Let's take a walk." He offered his arm.

I paused, staring at the outstretched arm and then back at his eyes. "I don't know if I should."

"I didn't do it." He swallowed, his eyes closing for a brief second before meeting mine again. "The rape? I'm sure you've heard about it by now. You can trust me. In fact, I'll even let you have one of the rape whistles."

"You carry them?" My eyes widened.

"Hey, guys get raped too." His smile fell, and then he reached into his pocket and handed me a whistle. "Don't forget the most important part about owning one of these babies."

"What?" I took the red whistle in my hands and examined it.

Weston's breath fanned my face. "Blow."

"Huh?" Okay, I was going to pass out. His lips were inches from mine.

"You have to blow..." His full lips expanded into a bold grin. "The whistle. You know, in order to get help."

"Oh," I said breathless. "Right."

He led me out of the lobby. I was lucky to be walking in straight lines after that little exchange. I had no idea why I'd captured his attention, but I still had that sinking feeling in the back of my mind that it wasn't a good thing. Being his friend would never work, and being more scared me half to death.

SEVEN

Note to self, when a girl's smile makes you forget your own name — you're in some deep shit.

Weston

"This way." I grabbed her hand and led her down the street. "So, tell me about yourself, Kiersten." Lame. My first question was so unoriginal I wanted to punch myself. That was what freshman orientation did to a person.

"I'm eighteen."

"No, I didn't—" I turned and found myself under the full force of her green eyes penetrating mine. "That is, yes, I'm glad you're over eighteen; I don't want to get in trouble for holding your hand or anything."

"Yeah, well, you don't strike me as the type of guy who just holds hands."

"You're right." I exhaled. "But I'm a fan of hands, or maybe it's just yours, Lamb." It was true. I liked her hands. Everything about her screamed innocence. I almost felt bad for corrupting her, for wanting her. Almost being the keyword.

"And there's the nickname."

"There it is," I agreed, then squeezed her hand more. We walked across the lawn and down to the sidewalk in silence. As we passed a few cars, the silence stretched out even further, then finally, beneath the second streetlamp, she stopped, tugging her hand back.

"Look…" She shifted nervously from foot to foot; her innocent eyes darted from the ground to my face. "I don't know what you're trying to do here. I appreciate your help and stuff today, but…"

Amused, I raised my eyebrows. "But?"

"I'm not like that," she whispered.

"Like what?"

"That." Her cheeks were stained pink. "I don't hook up with guys."

"Oh, that." I grinned at her embarrassment. "I don't either."

"Huh?"

"Hook up with guys. I'm not like that. So now that we've had that particular conversation, we can be friends." I reached for her hand again.

"I, uh—" She wasn't able to finish her sentence because one of my teammates had the worst timing in the universe and just happened to drive by.

"Michels!" he shouted out his window. "Party at Kappa tonight!" He honked his horn and peeled out.

"Friends?" she asked.

"Worse." I chuckled. "Teammates." I stopped walking and touched her arm lightly. "You want to go to a different party?"

"I should probably get back—"

"Come." I pulled her closer to me. "Just for a few minutes. I'll introduce you to some upperclassmen, get you some milk, and have you tucked into your bed safely by midnight."

Her eyes narrowed.

"Fine, I'll have you tucked in alone. As in, without me."

Kiersten looked down the street. "Fine. Thirty minutes and don't think I won't use the rape whistle!"

"Please," I whispered. "Then when you return it, I'll know exactly what it feels to have your lips blowing across mine."

She flinched. "You can't say things like that to me."

"Why?" I tilted her chin toward my face. "Does it make you uncomfortable?"

"Yes," she whispered.

"Fine." I sighed. "I'll just think them and look longingly in your direction every few minutes, sound good?"

She laughed. "Whatever makes you happy."

"Whistles." I nodded. "And redheads." I reached for her hand again. "Virgins." Interesting, her blush deepened as her hand clenched mine tighter. I was good at reading people, and I'd bet my entire fortune she'd never even been kissed. It was why it made her uncomfortable. "Virgin lamb…" I sighed. "I may just sacrifice you on the altar."

"I'd rather not be sacrificed."

"You never know." I gave her a cocky grin, "You may like it."

"You never know." She sighed dreamily. "I may stab you."

"Fair." I chuckled. "Now, let's go. People to see, milk to drink, freshmen to corrupt."

EIGHT

Things are never as they seem—ever.

Kiersten

'd never been to a frat house. My only experience in even knowing what they looked like could be traced to the movies. You know, guys partying, people drinking, cups littering the lawn.

What I didn't expect was actual order.

The music was loud, but the spread was insane.

Alcohol was everywhere, food was everywhere, people were dressed like movie stars, and every single guy looked like he'd just stepped from a magazine.

"Guys," Weston put his hands on my shoulders and urged me forward, "This is Kiersten."

"Hey," a few of them mumbled in greeting and smiled. They didn't look like your typical jocks. In fact, most of them were sipping their drinks and discussing football, while the girls around them were happily chatting about classes.

"Oh…" Weston tugged my hand. "And those guys over there who just walked in…" He pointed in the direction of two pretty big guys. One had black-rimmed glasses and a goatee; the other was at least six-foot-seven and lanky. Both appeared to be in their mid-thirties. "They work for me. Or my dad. However you look at it. You have any issues? Anyone bothers you here? You run toward them with the whistle, got it?"

"Uh, sure, but why would anyone bother me?"

Someone chuckled behind me. "Fresh meat."

"Need I say more?" Weston groaned. "Meet Drake."

"Hi, Drake." I swallowed, trying really hard to not meet his predatory gaze. He had dark brown eyes and sandy blond hair.

He nodded. "'Sup."

And that was the end of the conversation.

Weston introduced me to tons of people, none of whom really cared who or what I was. Mainly they were polite, but that was it. After a few more introductions, he took me into the kitchen. "Lets' get you a drink."

"Oh, I've never drunk before." I held up my hands.

"I know." Weston chuckled. "Which is why you and I are on a mission of sorts. First frat party, first drink, first time with a senior—"

"I'm good." I shook my head at the cup he held out to me.

"Not yet, you're not. One sip, and then I can die happy." His smile didn't reach his eyes as he held out the cup and waited.

"Ugh, peer pressure. You know, you're the worst RA I've ever met, right?"

He shrugged.

The liquid sloshed in the cup. It was dark and smelled like rotten bananas. "What is this?"

"Beer. One sip. Go."

I plugged my nose. He laughed, but I didn't care. It tasted like bitter bananas and mold, and after one sip, I was done. I coughed and gave him back the cup.

"See?" His smile was contagious. "Was that so hard?"

"It was awful!" I smacked him on the arm.

"What did I tell you? No whistle! See, I'm safe, promise." He laughed and then stumbled a bit on his feet. With a curse, he grabbed the counter.

"Are you okay?" I rushed to Weston's side.

He jerked away from me and blinked a few times. "Yeah, fine. I just… I need to go grab something from James. I'll be right back, okay? Don't follow anyone upstairs and no drinking anything, not even water."

"Yes sir." I saluted, trying to make him laugh. Instead, he looked like he was going to puke as he walked slowly out of the kitchen, leaving me alone.

"Interesting," a female voice said a few minutes later. "You his new project?"

I turned around. "Project?"

The girl was gorgeous. Her legs went on forever, she had a tight white dress on, and her black hair hung in loose curls around her chest. "Yup, project." She grabbed a cup of beer and drank. "He picks a freshman every year."

"He does?" Dread filled my stomach.

"What can I say? He gets bored easy. Believe me, by Christmas he'll have forgotten your name and moved on to the next girl. Let me guess, small town? Innocent? Everything a powerful guy like Wes is attracted to, but nothing he would actually go home to if you get my meaning. He saves as many as he can and then parties with the ones who actually give a shit about him and his life. So enjoy it while you can. I know I did." She took another long sip and laughed just as Weston walked back into the room.

The minute his eyes fell on the girl, I could have sworn he snarled. "What. The. Hell. What are you doing here, Lorelei?"

"I was invited," she purred. "You should be happy to see me. It's good press. You and I talking like nothing happened."

His hands clenched at his sides. "But it did."

"Says who?" She threw her head back and laughed. "I was just getting to know your new little friend here."

"And we were just leaving." Weston grabbed my arm and pulled me closer to him.

"Remember what I said, freshman." Lorelei eyed me one last time and waltzed out of the room. I exhaled and followed Weston as he steered me out of the house. The two guys he'd pointed out earlier trailed us a few hundred feet behind as we walked down the same street we'd just come up.

"I know you don't know me." Weston's words were clipped as if all his joy had just been sucked out of him. "But you can't trust anything that girl says. She's trouble. Let's just put it that way. She's not even supposed to be within ten miles of me, let alone ten feet."

"Is she a student here?"

"Nah." He laughed without humor. "Graduated a year ago. Our parents were close."

"Were?"

"Yeah." His head jerked down as he cursed and bit down on his lip. "Until everything went down last year. They still think I did it. Doesn't help that Lorelei's a struggling actress. The one and only time I ever saw her succeed in selling a part was when she was trying to put me in jail for something I didn't even do."

"I'm sorry." My heart clenched in my chest.

Weston sighed. "Don't be. What's done is done, right?"

"Right," I murmured.

"I'm not feeling very well." He stumbled a bit. "I think I may be catching something, so I'm going to walk you nicely to your room and then say goodnight."

"Have it all planned out, do ya?" I teased.

He actually laughed. Wow, his face lit up when he was happy. I wanted to be the reason he laughed, even though I knew it was ridiculous. I hardly knew the guy, and what I did know told me he probably wouldn't be the best person for me to hang out with.

"Kiersten?"

"Yeah?" The party was still raging by the time we walked into the building and got on the elevator.

"Thanks."

"For what?" My breathing seemed erratic as his eyes focused on my lips for a few seconds before looking back toward the elevator doors.

"For believing me."

I reached for his hand. What was I doing? I clenched his fingers in mine. "Until you give me a reason not to trust you, I'll always believe you. It's what people do."

"Blindly trust complete strangers?" His focus was elsewhere. His eyes had glazed over, and he looked really pale.

"Nah." We walked down the hall to my room. "Make friends and believe them when they tell the truth."

"Kiersten…" Voice gruff, he leaned against my door. "I don't want to be your friend."

"Oh." I hated how my stomach dropped to my knees like

he'd just told me he hated Christmas and wanted to burn every last romance book on my Kindle.

"More," he whispered, and this time I could feel the heat from his lips on my ear as he talked. "With you, I think I'll always want more. But—" He sighed and held out his hand. "I'll settle for friends, that is, if the offer still stands."

Fingers tingling, I reached for it and shook. His smile lit up my world. It shattered my previous existence, and again the same eerie feeling washed over me. Like I was running out of time, or maybe like the darkness was coming again. I tried to pull free, but he held me there.

I hated that feeling of losing control. Usually, the meds helped, but right then, it was like his eyes were asking me to jump into the blackness with him, and I wasn't so sure I was ready for that.

"It's going to be okay," he whispered, taking a piece of my hair from the ponytail and examining it.

"What is?"

"Your first day of class." A sad smile crossed his face. "What else would I be talking about?"

"Oh, you know… life," I joked, trying to get his other smile back.

"Right." His smile faded as he swallowed hard. "Well, sweet dreams, Kiersten. Think of me."

"And your eight-pack?" I offered.

He threw his head back and laughed. "Wow, I needed that. Thanks. Friend."

"Anytime…" I fought to keep myself from touching him "Friend."

"I think you may be the best friend I've ever had." He didn't move. Instead, he watched me, and his eyes seemed to take in every detail about me as if I was going to disappear or something.

"That's a good thing, right?"

"I wish I knew." He pointed down the hall. "My room beckons me, as does a five a.m. practice. Night."

NINE

A gift? A curse? Who knew... but time was running out.

Weston

I groaned over the toilet, losing all my breakfast, lunch, dinner, and the protein shake I'd just choked down. I hated throwing up. It made me feel like a little kid all over again. My mom had always been there when I was sick.

Now it was just my dad.

And he sent people to do his dirty work. Not that he didn't love me, he just had bigger things to deal with than his son tossing up his cookies. I was glad I was sick all night. It meant I was getting it out of my system before practice. Even on my worst day, I was still better than half the guys out there.

I shouldn't have pushed myself so hard, especially after the new round of meds, but I'd wanted to help Kiersten. Her innocence called to me, just like her darkness. Damn, but I could almost see the dark cloud billowing over her head. I'd lived through that and more. Sometimes her smile was fake;

other times, she was so damn concerned with what others thought about her that I wanted to shake her. Maybe from the outside it didn't appear that way, but her eyes, the way they would focus on everything almost as if taking too long to stare at something might bring attention to her. It was weird, seeing a girl who physically screamed look at me, cower into herself.

Friends? Hell no. I was probably the worst idea for her, the worst friend in the entire universe. I'd end up breaking her heart regardless. So I knew I may as well make it as painless as possible. Since I was clearly lacking in the self-control department, I'd be the best damn friend she ever had. I just couldn't attach myself romantically. I wouldn't do that to her. After all, she had a full, happy four years of school left, whereas I was *done* in a few months.

I threw on my practice jersey and grabbed my keys. I hated walking to practice. It was wet in the mornings; the university was right on the Pacific Ocean, meaning it was always cold this early.

With a sigh, I made a stop at Kiersten's dorm room and slid a note under her door.

"And so begins the friendship," I whispered. Maybe I could help her crawl out of that damn cocoon. Maybe it would be enough to leave a smile on my face when I left for good.

TEN

Maybe the darkness wasn't closing in like I first assumed.
Maybe, I just invited it without knowing?

Kiersten

The alarm jolted me awake. The first thing I realized was that my nightmares hadn't been as terrible last night. In fact, I didn't wake up screaming. I wanted to jump into the air and thank God. The medication had been giving me nightmares for months now, but it was worth it if it helped me power through the day.

I turned off the alarm on my phone and shuffled to the door. I was thankful that I had been put in a suite with Lisa. We shared a kitchen and living room with two other girls who were pre-med. Which meant it was like living alone. They didn't watch TV, they didn't live, and when I asked if they were on Facebook, I got judgmental looks from both of them.

I yawned and went to start making coffee in the kitchen just as Lisa tumbled out of her room, swearing. "Too early!"

"It's seven."

"My point exactly." She ran her hands through her blond hair and sat at the table. "Where were you last night? I came home, and you were already in bed."

"I was, uh…" I busied my hands, pouring the grounds into the filter. "With Weston. He took me to another party and—"

"Whoa!" she croaked. "Another party? Where at?"

"Kappa," I said.

"NO way!" she screamed. "They have the best parties! Only upperclassmen are invited! Did you meet anyone hot? Were they nice? Did they have drugs? I've heard they have drugs. Holy crap, are you going to go back? Should you go back? We need Gabe."

"You done?"

She inhaled and exhaled twice before nodding. "Yes, I think so."

"Good." The coffee started brewing. "Everything seemed normal. It was just a few gorgeous people drinking, eating, and—" I left out the part about Lorelei.

"And?" Lisa scooted closer to the table. "And what? He kissed you? You're having his love child? He wants to marry you, and I get to live above the garage?"

"No." I laughed. "To all of the above. He wants to be friends."

"Friends?" She tapped her mouth with her fingertip. "With the hottest guy on campus? Why does that rub me the wrong way?"

"Because you want in his pants."

Lisa snorted. "Honey, I'd *be* his pants. That's how desperate I am. But why friends? Why not more?"

"He's not into freshmen." I shrugged.

"Ri-i-i-i-ight." Lisa nodded. "But he is male, and you're hot. That means one thing."

"You're living above his garage?"

"I wish." She pouted and looked toward the door. "What's that?"

"The door?" Seriously, did she drink last night?

"Thank you." Lisa rolled her eyes. "Not that." She pointed at the door. "That."

A piece of paper was folded on the floor. It had my name on it. Holy crap! My name, in really nice handwriting.

"It's not like it has anthrax in it." Lisa bent down and picked it up. "Read it." She thrust it in my face. "Come on! I'm curious."

The coffee pot dinged. I snatched the paper and went to pour us both cups of coffee. Once seated, I tore into the note and read.

> *People don't write letters anymore... such a shame, don't you think? Day 1. Your mission, if you choose to accept it: Make two new friends, you know, people other than your roommate and her cousin. I don't count either. Be sure to smile really big and raise your hand at least once in class. I'll see you at lunch.*
>
> *Your friend—Wes.*

My smile couldn't get any bigger if it tried. I re-read the note, again and again; each time I read it, my heart pounded harder in my chest. It was the first morning in two years that I wasn't thinking about my past. In fact, I hadn't thought once about my parents' accident. I was too happy, too excited to think about anything but the fact that a guy had written me a letter.

"Well?" Lisa asked. "What's it say?"

"I'm getting married!"

"WHAT?" She screamed.

"Kidding," I said, laughing as I held out the note. "Here, it's from Wes."

"Oh, so now it's Wes?" Her eyebrows arched.

"Uh…" I looked away. "I meant Weston."

"Right," she grumbled and started reading. Her smile grew just like mine had, and by the time she was done, she looked up, tears of excitement in her eyes. "He wrote you a love note!"

"It's more of an instruction card." I waved her off. "Clearly, he's trying to push me out of my shell."

"Well, you are kind of like a hermit. And you did grow up in—" She paused. "What's the name of that rock you lived under? The one with one store?"

I sighed. "Bickelton."

"Right. There." She shook her head. "You need to get out and live. Methinks that Weston Michels thinks so too…"

"But—" I didn't want to sound lame. Insecurity won over, making my voice shaky. "Why me?"

"Why *not* you?" She threw the letter onto the table. "You're beautiful, and you sparked his interest. Does there have to be a reason?"

"There's always a reason," I explained. "Guys like that don't just pay attention to girls like me."

"Girls like you are the reason guys like him exist." Lisa smiled warmly. "You don't see yourself how others see you. Maybe he sees more than you do when you look in the mirror. Whatever it is, don't brush him off. He's making an effort, and if I were you, I'd say thank you to God in my prayers tonight."

I smiled. "Maybe I will."

"Great." She stood abruptly and stretched. Something glittered beneath her shirt — was that a belly ring? "Now, let's get ready for our first class!" She did a little dance and ran off to her room, leaving me with my coffee and my note.

ELEVEN

Drugs suck. Getting hit by a three-hundred-pound lineman?
Yeah, sucks way harder.

Weston

"**M**ichels!" Coach Jackson yelled. "Where's your head this morning, huh? Focus!"

Right. Focus. Stop thinking about red hair and mega-watt smiles and what that smile would feel like if it was directed at me again, and that red hair again running through my hands, and—

"Michels!" The football snapped just in time for me to grab it and finish the play. I seriously needed to stop getting so distracted by her. What the hell was wrong with me?

By the time practice finished, I had enough bruises to last me a lifetime, not the best sign for a quarterback.

"Where were you today?" Brad asked, throwing off his clothes and jumping into the shower.

"Not present," I grumbled, doing the same.

"Right." He snorted. "Better get present if we want that bowl game this year."

I hated talking about the future. What was the point anyway? I nodded and gave him a gruff. "Yeah, you're right."

Once I was done showering, I went to one of the many school coffee shops and grabbed a protein shake. Two classes, and then I could see Kiersten. She would have read my note by now, so she was either pissed or smiling. I hoped she was smiling. In fact, I hoped that when she woke up and read the note, she'd forget all about how to frown.

"**L**unch." I pushed a pile of food toward Kiersten and watched for a minute as she examined it with distaste. "You have to eat."

"Not hungry." She pushed the tray away and crossed her arms over her stomach.

"Bad first few classes?"

She glared.

I held up my hands. "Wanna talk about it?"

"I can't." Her face flushed as she looked around the cafeteria. Most everyone was staring at us as if we'd just announced we were going to adopt one of Brad Pitt's twenty children.

"I'll take care of it." I sighed and sent a quick text to James. He hated covering for me, but at least it got people to stop gawking. I watched him across the cafeteria. He looked at his phone, scowled, and then threw his newspaper onto the table. In an instant, he was walking toward us; after two or three strides, he collapsed onto the floor.

Everyone gasped.

"Okay, so now they aren't staring." I nodded to Kiersten, "What happened in class?"

"Is he all right?" She pointed at James.

"Low blood sugar." I looked away for a brief moment and cleared my throat. "So, class?"

"Should we, like, call someone?" She pulled out her cell. I grabbed her wrist and shook my head. "He'll be fine in about ten minutes or as long as it takes for you to tell me your story."

"O-okay." She kept staring at James, but at least she was talking. "I raised my hand in class, but the professor reprimanded me for correcting him."

I winced.

"And I made two new friends."

I smiled.

She didn't.

"Let's just say they're a bit more friendly than you."

I swear I saw two deaths by my hands. "Who were they? Did they touch you? Hurt you? I'll kill them, seriously. I'll—" I stood and started frantically looking around the cafeteria for any punk freshman that was staring at her cross-eyed.

"Sit down." She pulled me to my seat and shook her head. "I told them I had a boyfriend, case closed."

"I meant friends who were girls." Blood roared in my ears. "Not guys."

"Well?" She threw her hands into the air in frustration. "They were the only two people that approached me."

"I bet they were," I grumbled.

"Wes?"

She called me Wes.

I could die happy.

Most people called me Wes. I hadn't told her it was okay. It seemed natural. It's how I'd signed my note.

I was turning into a chick.

My smile grew as her eyes narrowed.

"What?" she asked.

"Nothing." I grabbed her hand and kissed it. "Just happy."

"That I failed at your little list?"

"No failure." I shook my head. "You tried, and that's what counts. You need to get out from underneath the cloud."

Her nostrils flared as she grabbed her bag and stood. "I gotta go."

"Sit."

"No."

"Sit." I jerked her down to the seat and softly held her hand in mine. I could feel her pulse in her wrist; it was erratic, angry. "I'm not sorry."

"I don't know what you're talking about."

"You remind me of my brother."

"Huh?"

"Coma. Died," I explained. "Overdosed."

"Gee, thanks," she said through clenched teeth.

I pushed back the dark thoughts of my brother's demise, barely holding it together by a thread. "Depressed, talented, awesome, my favorite person in the world… he was all those things. And you — you remind me of him. I don't know why, but you just do. So yeah, I'm pushing a little, but I think you can take it. Tell me you're strong enough to take it."

"You don't know me." Her voice was hard. It had an edge to it that I wasn't used to hearing from girls.

"I do."

"You. Don't."

I released her hand. "Better than you realize. Look, I don't sugarcoat things, and I sure as hell don't have time to be that guy. The one who waits for weeks to finally crack all your defenses. I'm different. Maybe I'm too intense. I get that. My methods are crazy. But I'm drawn to you — and honestly, you need me."

"I don't need anyone," she whispered, sounding like she hardly believed herself, let alone was capable of convincing anyone else.

"You do," I said. "And I'll wait until you say it to my face if that's what it takes for you to realize it."

With that, I got up from my seat and left her. I'd keep writing my notes. I'd keep pushing her.

Maybe if I could save her — I let out a rugged breath… maybe in saving her, I'd be saving him. I couldn't then, but I can now.

TWELVE

People should just mind their own business. Right?
I mean, how am I his problem?

Kiersten

"**W**ho the hell does he think he is?" I yelled into the phone.

Uncle Jo sighed heavily on the other line. "He sounds like a nice young man, and he does have a point."

I wanted to throw something against the wall. I pulled out another pill and crunched it between my teeth. It was bitter, but I didn't care. I needed to feel better. I mean, in theory, I knew antidepressants weren't supposed to be taken like that, but the placebo effect was enough — for now.

"Kiersten, he was being a good friend. You do tend to wear your emotions on your sleeve."

"I've known him a day! And what? He wants to help me? To save me? He's making it worse!"

"How so?" Uncle Jo asked in a calm voice. "It seems to me

that he's pulling off the band-aid you've been gluing to your feelings. I'm no expert, but you can only function at the level you've been functioning at for so long. I allowed you to go to school four hours away so that you could have your freedom. Remember our agreement."

"Yeah, yeah." I sat on the bed and groaned. "Shape up, or you ship out and pack my crap."

His chuckle calmed me. "Exactly. You haven't dealt with your grief in a healthy way. You shouldn't still be on antidepressants; you shouldn't be so uptight. For God's sake Kiersten. You're eighteen!"

"I'm ancient."

"You're a kid." I could just see him pacing on the floorboards in the kitchen. "Live. Go have a beer — and only one. Cheat death, like they didn't. Go streaking through your dorm. Do something. Anything's better than you staring at the damn wall like you've been doing for the past two years."

"You been watching Dr. Phil?" I asked.

"Maybe." He laughed. "The point is you have to live."

It was the first time someone had given me permission to do exactly that. I always felt like I had to suffer because they did. How stupid, right? But the human condition is stupid. We torture ourselves in order to feel better — that's what I was doing. Torturing myself because it wasn't fair.

"Stop," Uncle Jo growled.

"What?"

"Thinking."

"I'm not—"

"You are." With a sigh, he spoke low into the phone. "Sweetie, your parents would have wanted you to do things, crazy things. They took risks. You torturing yourself and being careful doesn't protect you from the bad."

And we get to the heart of the matter.

I was terrified. I felt like I had to control everything. If I controlled what I ate, what I wore, how I acted, who I spoke to, I could keep myself from the same fate.

"They loved you," he said forcefully.

Words lodged in my throat.

"They would want you to live."

I swallowed the emotion in my throat. "But what if I don't live? What if I die?" I could feel the darkness starting to overwhelm me. I sat on my bed and put my head between my knees. The doctor always said anxiety was a form of depression. I'd never believed him, but for the past two years, anxiety and depression had been my only friends. Maybe that's why Wes was pushing me.

"Live," Uncle Jo rasped. "Mess up. Get arrested. Hell, get caught doing drugs."

I laughed at his exaggeration

"I just want to know you're okay."

"I'm okay, Uncle Jo, I promise. You know you're the worst parent ever, right?"

He sighed and then chuckled. "Or the best, however you want to look at it."

"You just told me to do drugs."

Silence and then, "Don't tell your grandma."

"Noted."

"All right, kiddo." Our time was almost up; he never talked long. He wasn't much of a talker, so tonight was kind of a shock. "Go do something stupid."

"Thanks, Uncle Jo, for talking."

"It's what I'm here for."

I hung up the phone and stared at my door. Do something stupid? Okay, fine. I was going to do something insane. Before I could change my mind, I stormed out of my room and took the next few flights of stairs to Wes's door.

My heart threatened to beat out of my chest as I knocked on the door once, twice, and then a third time.

"Hold up," his voice called from inside.

The door swung opened. His smile grew from small to ginormous.

"I'm done with my list."

"I know you told me earlier."

"I made my own." I lifted my chin in defiance.

"Did you now?" He crossed his arms and chuckled, leaning his large muscled body against the door frame. "And what's yours say?"

"I can't tell you."

His brow furrowed.

"I have to show you."

"Okay," he said slowly. His eyes closed just slightly as a sexy grin spread across his face. "So show me."

Crap. I was sweating. I couldn't punk out. Uncle Jo wanted crazy? I'd give him crazy. I stood up on my tiptoes and brushed my mouth against Wes's. I was so nervous that my lips were actually trembling when they touched his; as soon as they made contact, I tried to pull back.

But Wes grabbed my chin between his fingers and pulled my face closer to his. "I have a list too, you know."

"Do you?" It was hard to breathe with him so close to me.

"Yup." His lips brushed mine again, and I felt his tongue push against the seam of my lips as if trying to break down my defenses, but I knew, the minute I opened up to him, I wouldn't be able to push him away anymore, and that scared the hell out of me.

"Open." He nipped at the corner of my mouth. "I won't hurt you."

But he already was; every moment spent in his presence was like getting a bucket of cold water thrown on me repeatedly. I didn't know what to believe or if I could trust him. Could you trust someone so beautiful? So talented? So perfect?

His hands moved from my chin to my shoulders and then ran down my arms causing chills to move across my body.

Wes blew lightly across my mouth. I gasped. And all was lost. He crushed his mouth to mine, his tongue massaging and tasting. I whimpered; he moaned low in his throat as his hands moved around my neck.

Next thing I knew, I was in his room, the door was slammed behind us, and his hands were resting at my hips. I rocked toward him, not really knowing what I wanted but needing to be closer to him.

Wes pulled away, his chest heaving with exertion. He swallowed, turned around, and cursed, "I'm sorry."

He was sorry? That he'd kissed me? I reached for the door, but the minute I pulled it open, he pushed it closed. I was facing away from him, his breath was hot on my neck, and soon his lips followed. I closed my eyes. It felt so good, him touching me. It was so right that I wanted to scream. I'd never felt so exposed to another person. I'd never felt such an adrenaline rush as when his tongue had touched mine or when his fingers grazed my hip bone.

"Stay," he whispered in a hoarse voice. "Stay with me."

"In your room?"

"No. On the roof." He chuckled in my ear. "Yes, in my

room. What if I promise not to touch you?"

"Isn't that what guys say before they seduce girls? At least in the movies?"

"Not a movie." His fingers tapped my collarbone and then moved slowly down the front of my shirt, stopping right on my heart. "I just want to feel your heart beating. That's all."

Was he trying to be romantic, or was he serious? His hand didn't leave my chest, and then I felt his body humming against mine as he pulled me back against him. "Please?"

"If I get kicked out of school—"

"You won't." He urged. "I'm the RA. You're in a fight with your roommate. I'm protecting your honor, all that stuff."

"Except my roommate kicks ass, you want to *steal* my honor, and you're a playboy."

"Playboy?" He removed his hand. "I guess so, but not with you."

"Yeah, so I'm different, huh? How many times have you told that to girls in the last twenty years?"

"It started when I was eight…" He began.

I laughed. I couldn't help it.

"Seriously." He turned me so I was facing him. "I'm not gonna lie. I want you. I want you so freaking bad that I'm pretty sure when I get to heaven I'm going to be sainted."

My eyes narrowed.

"Things just…" He cursed and ran his fingers through his dark blond hair. "Things just feel better with you around. More complete. Does that make sense?"

"I guess." I wasn't ready to admit to him that I was falling hard and fast. I mean, I'd known him, what? Two days?

"Besides…" He sighed. "You came to my room, remember?"

"My uncle said to do something crazy."

He held up his hands. "Anytime you feel the urge, I'm here. In fact, I may have to remind you of this conversation every five minutes or so; hope you don't mind."

"Thanks." I gulped and shoved my hands into my pockets.

"So, we should sleep."

"What? No painting each other's nails and wearing face masks?" I joked.

He threw his head back and laughed. "Well, it'd probably get my focus off of tossing you against the wall and taking every last shred of your innocence. So yeah, maybe I should paint your nails, then I can imagine that you're not standing in front of me with swollen lips and tousled red hair. Damn, I love your hair." He reached for a few pieces and sighed.

"Maybe this is a bad idea." I started backing away.

Wes grabbed my hand. "Good. I like bad ideas; they make me feel alive."

"And you need to feel more alive than you already do?"

His face fell. He looked down at the ground and whispered, "You have no idea."

THIRTEEN

If she only knew... then again, she'd probably murder me in my sleep. I'd rather die by her hands than... well, never mind.

Weston

"**S**o we doing this or not?" I changed the subject.

She looked at the door, then back at me, then back at the door. Making the decision for her, I twisted the lock and pulled out a pair of boxers and a t-shirt for her to wear. "We don't have bathrobes in this fancy establishment, but I do have clean clothes for you to sleep in. Now strip."

"Wh-hat?"

"Kidding." I laughed, though a part of me had to admit I'd been hopeful. "The bathroom's just through there. Go change; I'll be sure to be fully clothed when you come back."

"Okay." Her hands were shaking. I reminded myself to send Uncle Jo a Christmas ham for his advice. On one hand, I was glad it led her to me, but on the other, had she decided to go to some other guy, I would have probably ended up in prison. So, maybe not a ham… A card? Sure, a card would be nice.

I quickly peeled off my shirt, threw on a pair of workout shorts, and lay on the bed. My dad had texted a few things about being nice to James and David. He also wanted to know how the new meds were. I was so sick and tired of medicine that I wanted to throw something against the wall. I was counting on Kiersten not being a snoop since my drug collection was happily displayed under my sink, not that she'd even know what the drugs were or how they worked. Even if she did an Internet search for the names, she'd be stunned to see over half of them were experimental.

"Ready." Kiersten's small voice called from the bathroom as the door opened and the light turned off. She was practically swimming in my clothes. I couldn't help the smile that spread across my face. She looked so damn sexy in my shorts; I wanted to charge toward her and rip them from her body.

Self-control.

I cleared my throat and patted the bed. "I don't bite."

"But you do lick."

"Always." I fought to keep my hands at my sides. Damn, but they itched to reach out and pull her against me. "I won't lick you now, Lamb."

"Says the wolf," she sang as she slowly made her way over to the bed and sat next to me. "I don't do things like this. Furthermore, I'm only doing this to prove a point to my uncle and myself."

"And what's that?"

"That I can live," she said in a low voice. "That I didn't die with them."

"Them?" I pulled her against my chest.

"I don't really talk about it much. Not unless you're a

doctor and charge over two hundred dollars an hour to scribble stuff on a notepad and prescribe me drugs." Her entire body tightened. "Not that I'm on drugs. I'm just—"

"Kiersten?"

"Yeah." She sounded like she was going to cry.

"It's fine to have help."

After a few moments of silence where her heartbeat slammed against my hand, she gave a jerky nod. "Thanks."

"You're welcome. Now, let's be all crazy and go to sleep."

"Like old people." She laughed.

"Yeah, exactly like that." Because if she squirmed any more against me, I was going to lose my mind. "Goodnight, Lamb."

"Night, Big Bad Wolf." She yawned and turned to face me. "I should warn you, sometimes I have night terrors."

"It's okay, I snore."

"Are you lying?"

"Yup."

She sighed and bit her lip. Damn, how I wanted to hold her lips captive like her teeth were.

"I peed the bed once."

Her eyes widened.

"I was four."

"How life-altering."

"It was." I nodded. "My teddy bear didn't make it."

"Tragic."

I shook my head. "I always wonder to myself, could I have done something different to save my bear?"

Her laugh made my heart skip a beat; in fact, it did a hell of a falter before going back to normal. "Thanks."

"For what?" I brushed some hair away from her porcelain face.

"Making me feel better."

"Well, I am your RA…"

"This probably isn't in the job description." She laughed. "And I know it wasn't in the brochure."

I shrugged. "Well, it's in the description now. My new job description is making you laugh and chasing away the bad dreams."

"I wish that was true."

"Sleep." I kissed her forehead. "And if you do any more crazy shit, can I be a part of it?"

"Sure, why?" Her eyelids fluttered closed.

Oh, you know, because I would murder anyone who touches you. "No reason; I just don't like to think of you being all crazy without your partner in crime."

"'Kay."

"Night.

"Night," she whispered.

FOURTEEN

Maybe I didn't dream because for once in my life,
I was living it.

Kiersten

"**M**orning, sunshine," a gravelly male voice said next to my ear.

I jolted awake and almost knocked my forehead against his. It was a close call. Wes jerked back and laughed, putting his hands behind his head as he stared up at the ceiling. "So, no nightmares."

"No nightmares." He seriously couldn't possibly know how life-altering it was to go through a full night without waking myself up screaming. Maybe it wasn't a side effect of the drugs. Maybe it was just me. Maybe I was defective.

"Class?" He yawned again.

I looked at the clock next to the bed. "In two hours. I should go."

"It takes you two hours to get ready? I had you more for a twenty-minute girl."

I slapped him across his hard stomach. "If you must know, I take thirty, but I want to get back before Lisa sends out a search party."

He was quiet for a moment and then asked, "Are you going to tell her where you were?"

"Maybe."

"I'll keep it a secret," he said. "Friends have secrets, right?"

"Right." I pushed away from the mattress and stood. It was the best night's sleep I'd had in two years. Part of me longed to return to the bed, to his warmth. Instead, I marched into the bathroom, changed back into my clothes from the day before, and grabbed my keys and phone.

"Same time tonight?" He winked, and dang, the man was sexy all stretched out on his bed. How the hell had I slept through that? With his body so close to mine? I must have been completely exhausted. Either that or I wasn't attracted to guys or something.

"Uh, I have homework."

"On day two of classes?" His eyebrows lifted, and then his face fell. "Oh, I see, you're going to do the whole avoiding thing. Well, let me shoot you straight. We didn't have sex, so you're not doing the walk of shame, things aren't awkward, and if you avoid me like the plague, I'll just stalk you."

"That's not creepy."

He shrugged.

I managed an eye roll and a smile as I unlocked the door and snuck out.

I made it all the way to the stairwell without anyone seeing me. Trying not to be loud, I padded down to my room and crossed the hall, just as Gabe came from the opposite direction. The grin on his face growing by the minute.

"Naughty girl, were you out all night?"

"Uh…" I looked away from him and tucked my hair behind my ears. "I fell asleep at the library."

He sighed. "I tried that excuse once. Apparently, they close at three a.m. and have security dogs check under the tables every night."

"Damn."

"Whoa, and a curse." He wrapped his arm around me and walked me down the hall to my room. "Someone walking on the wild side?"

This time I rolled my eyes without any effort.

He paused, releasing his hold on my arm, and then his nose was in my hair, on my neck, everywhere.

Too much in shock to do anything, I froze.

Gabe pulled back. A smug grin plastered all over his chiseled face. "Sex. I smell sex on you."

Guilt slapped me across the face. I tried to hide it, but Gabe saw it. He nodded once and then tapped his finger against his mouth. "My money's on Michels."

And heat just exploded across my face.

"In his room?"

I started fidgeting with my keys so I could unlock the door. Gabe grabbed my hand and held it captive. "A word of warning." His eyes lost all hint of teasing. "He's probably not the type of guy to get involved with for your first—"

Now Gabe was blushing right along with me.

"My first?" I straightened tried my best to look ignorant.

"Just your first." He swore and put the key in the lock. "He's rich. Women want him. Hell, my grandma wants him. Just — just be careful. Guys like that, they don't do commitment. They do one night stands."

"Funny," I said with a snort. "That's exactly what Lisa said about you."

"Hey!" He twisted the key and pushed the door open for me to go through. "I don't pretend to be innocent, okay? I screw girls, they say thank you, and I let them go on their merry way. Both parties satisfied, end of story. I'm upfront about what I am and who I am…"

"And he isn't?"

"He's secretive," Gabe swore. "And I know he didn't rape that girl. I'm just saying, to be careful, that's all."

"Careful?" Lisa's sleepy voice came through the bedroom door, and then she appeared in short white shorts and a tank top. "Who has to be careful?"

I shot Gabe a pleading look. He sighed guiltily. "I do. I totally got drunk and almost bagged your roommate last night."

Lisa screamed.

Gabe smiled. "At least you're awake now."

"Don't scare me like that!" She swatted him on the arm. "She's too pure for your blood."

"Don't I know it," he murmured and sent me a wink while I mouthed a thank you.

"Breakfast." I pressed my hand to my forehead and ran my fingers through the front part of my hair. "Why don't I make everyone breakfast?"

"Sure." Lisa yawned and stretched. "I'm gonna go shower real quick."

After she left, Gabe tilted his head in my direction. "So, is this a breakfast or a guiltfest?"

"Hilarious."

He grinned and lifted his hands into the air. He looked

like a buffer version of Adam Levine with his ripped white shirt, tattoos, and skinny jeans.

"What?" his eyes narrowed.

"Nothing." I felt my cheeks blush. Well, I was officially a hussy. "You just look nice."

"Nice?" he repeated.

I nodded.

"Nice?" He leaned against the counter and crossed his arms. "Hmm, never been called nice before. You sure Michels didn't addle your brain after your crazy night of—"

"—talking and sleeping," I interrupted.

Gabe snorted. "Really? That's all that went down? Hmm, didn't know he was gay."

"He's not." I smirked and then realized I was caught.

"Oh?" Gabe nudged me with his elbow. "And how do we know that?"

"Er, because he has a reputation."

The room was silent for a bit while I mixed some of the pancake batter together and then turned on the stove.

"Good kisser?" Gabe asked.

The skillet fell out of my hands, clattering against the stove. Gabe's chuckle made me want to stab him with a fork.

He held up his hands in mock innocence. "Just a question."

"Yes." I licked my lips. "He is. But it was more like a dare to myself. He didn't start it. I did."

"Nice." Gabe took the batter from my hands and continued mixing while I went to the fridge and pulled out some OJ. "You telling me that underneath that sweater and frigid interior is a sex kitten just pawing her way out?"

I chose not to answer, instead busying myself with pouring

juice into the three glasses and making sure the pan was sprayed for the pancakes.

"Want to make funny shapes and freak Lisa out?" Gabe asked. Clearly, we were done talking about me. I couldn't be more thankful.

"She's scared of pancakes?"

"Mickey Mouse ones." His eyes twinkled with humor. "Tragic experience at Disneyland when she was four."

"Wait." I laughed. "She's scared of Mickey?"

"He sneezed in her face. Her princess hat fell off. She cried. It was a whole..." he waved in the air, "...episode."

"Sure." I grabbed the spoon. "I used to make these all the time for—" My voice trailed off.

"For?" he said.

"For my family."

"Cool." He dropped it and went to get plates while I dropped the batter onto the hot skillet.

Lisa finished showering just as we made the last pancake. Gabe chuckled and rubbed his hands together. "It's the little things in life that thrill me."

"Good to know." I put a pancake on Lisa's plate and handed it to him.

"Cousin?" Gabe called. "We made you something extra special."

"Mm." She took a deep appreciative sniff. "It smells like pancakes, yeah?" She placed the dish on the table and pulled out her chair. Then her eyes fell on her plate. With a scream, she stepped back and tripped over her chair, sailed to the ground, and landed with a thud.

"Classic." Gabe held out his fist. I bumped it.

"Damn, mouse," Lisa said from the floor.

Gabe went to help her up. She swatted his hand away. "Lisa, don't mope."

"I'm not moping." She crossed her arms. "I'm just… on pancake strike."

He sighed and knelt down. "Want me to break up your pancake, so it doesn't look mousey anymore?"

"I don't care, do what you want," she snapped.

Gabe reached for her plate and destroyed the mouse shape, then handed it back. "See? All better."

Lisa kissed his cheek and allowed him to help her up. "Thanks, Gabe."

"It was a mouse." I was still processing the fact that she'd been that freaked out over a pancake.

"Don't even go there." Lisa thrust her finger in my face. "You have night terrors and scare your roommate crapless. I hate Mickey. We all have our hang-ups." She had me there.

"Night terrors?" Gabe tilted his head in my direction. "Don't only little kids have night terrors?"

"And me." I plopped down onto my seat. "Apparently." Though I hadn't had one last night. I left that part out. It was a rarity.

Once we finished eating, I sent Uncle Jo a quick text.

> I kissed a guy and ate way too many pancakes this morning. How's that for crazy?

He replied back right away.

> That's my girl.

FIFTEEN

Whoever invented trial drugs should be shot — or maybe just me. Yeah, forget him, shoot me.

Weston

"When did the nausea start?" David felt my forehead and grimaced. "A few hours ago? Days?"

I pushed his hand away and cursed. "I think the better question would be, when haven't I felt nauseous? Seriously, I'm all better now, see?" I gave him a wide smile and stood. I had to brace myself against the desk for a few brief moments before I felt like I was solid enough to walk in a straight line.

David stood right along with me. "We have to record these things, Wes. You know that."

I groaned and made my way to the door. "I know that. It's been the same for the past six months, and I hate to break it to you, but I'm not getting better."

"That's a bad attitude, and you know it. The doctor said—"

"Screw the doctors!" I hit my fist against the door as my voice wavered with frustration.

I felt David's heavy sigh. I was used to those. The last year had been filled with them. First, my dad's sigh at learning that the drugs were our last option, my coach's sigh when I told him I might not be able to finish out the year, and finally the doctor's sigh when he said my chances were at fifty percent.

"Look." My lips felt so damn dry. A side effect from the meds, I licked them and sighed. "I'm sorry, it's just been a rough day. Make the damn note. I feel nauseated, my vision is blurred a bit, and I puked this morning."

Silence, and then I heard scribbling. "Anything else?" David asked.

"Yeah." I grabbed my keys from the desk. "I'm going out, don't wait up—"

"But—"

"Please," I pleaded. "I need normal right now."

"Fine," David swore under his breath. "Just keep your cell on, and if you feel funny at all, you come straight back to the dorm, all right?"

"Yup." I waltzed out.

I really was a joke of an RA. I'd been in my room all but thirty minutes the second day of classes. I'd wanted the job though. Scratch that; I needed it. Just like I needed a normal minute. The dean about shit himself when my dad went into his office, guns blazing. I'd never been more proud.

Most people probably assumed the worst, that I'd been demoted to an RA position to make up for the previous year.

Truth? I begged for it.

Coach had been pissed, but at least my dad understood. I told him I wanted to help the new kids, show them the ropes, but really it was about my brother. He'd died his freshman year of college, and I wasn't about to leave this world allowing that to happen to someone else.

Which is why I stopped on Kiersten's floor.

I wasn't sure if she'd be back from class yet, but it was worth a shot. I knocked twice on her door and waited.

After some arguing and shuffling, the door opened.

It was Gabe, the cousin, maybe my competition. I wasn't sure. He gawked at me for a minute, and then a grin spread across his features. "Sleep well last night?"

"Better than you." I smiled.

He nodded. "I believe it."

"Kiersten?"

"Homework."

"On the second day?" I pushed past him and let myself in.

Gabe raised his hands. "All I know is she said she had homework, and she's in her room. She only had two classes today, both morning ones."

"Good to know I'm not the only one stalking her," I grumbled.

At Gabe's smug grin, I clenched my hand into a fist and went to knock on her door. "Kiersten?"

Sniffling. I heard sniffling, and then something dropped. To hell with that. I burst in.

Wow, I really should have waited for her to open the door. She was naked.

Well, not entirely naked, but it sure as hell looked like it. She was wearing yoga pants and a sports bra. And I was sporting a grin so wide I'm sure I looked possessed.

"Hey!" Gabe called from the hallway. I slammed the door in his face and locked it.

"Oh, I feel safe now," Kiersten mumbled, rising from the yoga mat. "Seriously, you can't just barge in on people."

"I'm so glad I did." I moved to the bed, scooted back, and leaned against the wall. "Continue."

She burst out laughing. "No. Not with an audience. I was working out, you pervert."

"I thought I heard you yelling my name. My mistake." I shrugged.

"Wow, all the way from the sixth floor, huh?"

"What can I say? It's a gift."

"Combine super-hearing with stalking, and you're a regular psycho."

My grin grew.

Kiersten jutted out her hip and put her hand on it. "I'm not working out in front of you."

"Then let's do it together."

Her eyes widened in horror.

That was a self-esteem booster if I'd ever seen one. "Not like that. I mean, let's go running."

"You run?"

I shook my head and spoke slowly. "I'm a quarterback. Of course, I run."

She blushed and put her hands on her face. "No, I mean, you run other than at practice."

"You never played sports, did you?"

She bared her teeth and shook her head no.

"We don't just work out in practice. I work out two hours a day on top of practice. Keeps me in shape. You know, gotta keep that eight-pack alive somehow."

"Will I ever live that down?" She sat on the floor and sighed.

"Lamb…" I teased. "Never."

"Fine. Let's run."

"Cool—"

"On one condition."

"Boo." I gave her a thumbs down.

"Hey!" She stood abruptly. "You haven't even heard my condition!"

"Okay, fine. You have five seconds."

"Patient, aren't you?"

"One…"

"Fine!" Kiersten grabbed a piece of paper from the desk and thrust it in my face.

I was just about to say *two* when the paper landed on my lap. With a sigh, I picked it up and started to read.

Ways to live, I read.

My heart clenched in my chest. Did she know about me?

1. Kiss a hot guy.

2. Go skinny dipping.

3. Finish one fruity drink with the little umbrella.

4. Read Pride and Prejudice all the way through.

5. Learn how to swim.

I paused. "You don't know how to swim?"

Kiersten's eyes flickered to the ground, so I kept reading.

6. Make two real friends.

7. Get off my antidepressants.

So I'd been right about one thing. She was depressed, but why? What girl, as perfect as Kiersten, would be depressed?

8. Go bungee jumping.

9. Eat cranberry sauce at Thanksgiving and try to eat a beet.

10. Fall in love.

11. Get heart broken.

12. Fall in love anyway.

I could help her! Oh, not with all of them. I mean, she couldn't fall in love with me. I wouldn't let her. It wouldn't be fair to either of us, and she was eighteen. I sighed and folded the paper back in half.

"So?" She twisted that glorious red hair around her fingers. "What do you think?"

"Let's do it."

Her face lit up like a Christmas tree. Before I knew what was happening, she'd charged toward me and wrapped her arms around my neck. Um, if that was the response I was going to get for helping her with a silly list, I was going to freaking buy her her own island before I... The thought died in my head. Ironic.

"You mean it? It's not weird? I'm not weird?"

I kissed her cheek. "Not weird, and I did tell you I wanted to help you with all things crazy, right?"

She nodded. A piece of lush red hair fell across her face meeting her flushed cheek like a caress.

"Good." I kissed her cheek again. Mainly because I could. "I say we can get most of this done before Thanksgiving."

"Really?"

"Absolutely." I helped her stand. "You know... minus the whole falling in love part."

Kiersten laughed. Damn, I loved that sound. "Right, well, I figured go big or go home."

"My kinda girl." With a wink, I put the paper back on her desk. "Now put on a shirt so guys don't lust after you. We, my dear, are going for a run."

SIXTEEN

At least running next to him meant I wasn't running from him; that was progress... right?

Kiersten

When Wes said we should go running, I mistakenly thought he meant jog. You know, as in go kinda slow, not like a bat out of hell.

The guy wasn't even talking.

But he was sweating.

So I guess it was a good trade-off, especially considering he'd opted to run without a shirt. I, however, had to look much less than sexy as I gasped for breath next to him.

"We're crossing something off your list right now, you know," he said in a perfectly normal voice.

My side sliced with pain as I wheezed out, "Oh yeah, what?"

"You want off your antidepressants."

"So you're..." I coughed. "Trying..." Holy crap, I was going to pass out. "...to kill me?"

"Negative." He chuckled. Seriously. How. Was. He. Breathing? "Studies show that hard exercise, the kind that evokes physical pain, actually releases happy chemicals in your brain, which heal emotional as well as physical pain. Kind of like a drug. Running is the quickest and most efficient way to get those happy chemicals in your body. You start running, and I guarantee that you'll feel better, possibly good enough to go off your drugs." He stopped running. Thank God.

I bent over and held up my hand. "I need a minute."

He patted my sweaty back and chuckled. "The thing is, Kiersten, drugs aren't bad. They're there to help you."

"They give me nightmares."

"So sleep with me."

"They make me feel weak." I exhaled another breath.

"Only because you're looking at it the wrong way."

I waited for his usual wisdom. Seriously, was the guy a shrink in another life?

"Just because you need help to cope doesn't make you any less strong. The truly weak people in this life are the ones who can't admit they need help. They're the ones who can't admit that they can no longer go at it alone. Those are the people who are weak. By asking for help, by taking help, you've just admitted your weakness, and in that, you find your strength. The weak of the world are those who think they've got it all figured out and flaunt it to others."

I paused a minute and then looked up. He was grinning from ear to ear.

"When did you get so smart?"

Wes shrugged as a bead of sweat ran down his jaw. "Lots of therapy. Believe me. You can't go to therapy your whole life and not walk away with at least a little good advice."

I snorted. "Clearly, I need to switch therapists."

"Great, because I take appointments, and dates are my currency, so pay up."

"Friends don't date."

He squinted against the sun and laughed. "Sure they do."

I bit down on my lip and told my heart to stop doing cartwheels across my chest. "That wasn't on my list."

"The date is."

"Is it?" I smiled. I couldn't help it. He was a freaking expert at peeling back all of my carefully erected walls.

"This weekend. Friday. You and me. Date."

I looked away, trying to at least make it appear like I wasn't ready to jump all over him and scream yes in his face. Of course, the guy had girls throwing themselves at him. Just walking with Wes got me weird stares and gaping looks from the entire female population.

"Okay," I said in a small voice. "But only as friends." I held out my hand to shake his.

He nodded and took my small hand captive in his. "At least you shake my hand now. A few days ago I was convinced I'd have to show you how like John Smith did to Pocahontas."

"Funny."

"Aren't I?" He chuckled and pulled my hand so that we were almost chest to chest.

"I'm sweaty."

"Yup."

"And I — I smell." Wow, way to scare him off.

Wes leaned in and sniffed the side of my head.

"Are you sniffing my skin?"

He shrugged. "You said you smelled. Just trying to prove you wrong."

"So I don't smell?"

"No…" He still hadn't moved his face. My breath quickened when I felt his intake of breath across my neck. "You smell, but it's a sweaty smell. I happen to like sweat."

"Charmer." My voice sounded airy and foreign.

And then a wet tongue touched just below my ear as his lips grazed the side of my face. "Absolutely."

Before I could slap him or push him away or roll my eyes, a ringing sounded. He stepped back and pulled out a sleek new iPhone. "What?"

I waited awkwardly while the smile fell from his face.

"No, it's fine. Not a problem. Yeah, I'll… I'll be there." He put the phone back in his pocket and zipped it up, then like a switch, he was happy again.

"You okay?" I crossed my arms.

"Fine, why?" He started walking back up the path toward the school.

"Phone call, sad face. You know, tension in your voice. That sort of thing."

"Oh. That." Wes didn't meet my gaze as we made our way through the last part of the trail and back onto school property. "No big deal, just drama with my dad, you know how parents can be. Sometimes they just annoy the hell out of you because they can."

I froze.

"Kiersten?" Wes touched my shoulder. "What's wrong?"

I opened my mouth, but all that came out was a gasp, and then I started running all over again.

Because the last time I'd talked to both my parents, we'd gotten into a fight, an epic fight, about me wanting to go to my first party as a sophomore in high school.

"Kiersten!" Wes called after me, but I kept running, focusing on the slap of my shoes against the cement. Left, right, left, right. I needed to get away.

I ran all the way up the huge concrete stairway that led to the dorms until finally, I collapsed onto the ground, scraping my knee in the process.

"Crap!" Blood trickled down my leg and pooled in my shoe. Tears burned at the back of my throat as I tried to keep myself from hyperventilating.

"Kiersten!" Wes was immediately by my side; he must have paced along behind me. He ripped part of my shirt and blotted the scrape alternating between blowing on it and trying to stop the bleeding. "What the hell was that? You scared the shit out of me. In fact, you're still scaring the shit out of me. What's wrong?"

I tried to jerk free from his grip, but he was too dang strong. I refused to meet his gaze.

"Talk to me." Wes's voice was gentle and coaxing. "I know it was something I said."

I nodded.

"About parents?"

I nodded again.

"What happened?"

"They're dead."

SEVENTEEN

And the Mr. Insensitive award goes to... Weston Michels.
I. Am. An. Ass.

Weston

What was I supposed to say to that? What could I say?

"It was an accident. You can rarely prepare for death, you know?" She shook her head.

Sadly, she wasn't right in that regard. You *could* prepare, and I knew from firsthand experience that it didn't make it any easier, but I wasn't about to tell her that. It wasn't the time.

"You were close to your parents?"

"As close as you can be in high school."

"What happened?"

I assumed it was a car crash or something sudden that took them.

"They drowned."

"What?" I sat down next to her on the concrete. "How?"

"Cave diving." She sighed. "They were risk-takers, unlike me. I was afraid of my own shadow until last year."

I chuckled and wrapped my arm around her.

"They were in Florida for another one of their diving trips. I don't know exactly what happened, but I do know they were careful. I never thought about the risks because they were always so safe." Her voice got really quiet. "I got in a huge fight with both of them over the phone. I wanted to go to a party, and they said no. I told them I hated them and didn't want to ever see them again."

Shit.

"They died three hours later. Their bodies were recovered miles inside the cave they were exploring. The safety ropes were tattered as if they'd been ripped in half. The police thought that maybe the surf came in sooner than my parents expected, causing the rope to rub against the sharp rocks."

Kiersten wiped at a few stray tears. "I can't imagine. It kills me to know that their last moments were spent lost in a dark watery hole. It's not as if you can go to the surface. It just seems so miserable, and I was powerless to do anything to stop them."

Risking getting myself slapped or worse, I licked my lips and said, "Kiersten, I think you're looking at it the wrong way." I could feel her muscles tense beneath my touch. It was as if I'd just told her I was going to hunt her, and I wanted her to run; every single part of her body pulled away, getting ready to bolt.

"Hear me out," I whispered. "They loved cave diving, right?"

"Yeah." Her voice was small and weak, but at least she was still sitting by me, not slapping or running.

"And they knew the risks involved in it?"

"Of course!"

"Close your eyes."

"What? No." She tried to pull away from me, but I held her firm.

"Kiersten, just close your eyes."

She shivered and huffed, then closed her eyes.

"Listen to my voice," I whispered against her ear. "Imagine the story differently. Your parents get off the phone with you, both irritated but not really upset. I mean, you were, what? Fifteen? All fifteen-year-old girls go through those stages."

"How would you know?"

"I'm a fifteen-year-old girl trapped inside this body." I chuckled against her ear. "And I know because I used to mentor at the youth center. Believe me, fifteen-year-old girls are terrifying."

Her shoulders relaxed.

"So they get off the phone with you, shake their heads, have a good sigh, and hold hands as they walk across the beach. They put on their gear, check and double-check their air and the ropes and then go into the cave. Something happens. Maybe it was just the perfect storm of the elements. The cave was so beautiful that they went farther and farther in, not realizing they didn't have enough air to get back. Or maybe they didn't realize the ropes were no longer attached to the way out."

Her breathing was erratic as I continued my story and rubbed her back. "Maybe they looked at their air, knew they didn't know which way to go, so just went one direction. Maybe, they grabbed hands and swam into the darkness, knowing full well that in a few minutes, they'd probably fall asleep. But at least they'd fall asleep holding hands. At least, the last thought in their heads would be of you, of their family, and at least they were with each other. I guess I don't look at their death the same way you do. You think of their death as torture. And I think of it as peace. Maybe that makes me crazy, but I can't imagine your parents, seasoned divers that they were, panicking and suffering." I shrugged. "I see them holding hands into the darkness, and I see them smiling."

Kiersten was silent for a while.

I pulled back to look into her eyes, but she was covering her face with her hands, and when she pulled back her fingers, they were wet with tears.

I didn't have time to prepare myself for her hug. She knocked me onto the concrete so fast all I could do was open my arms to her and hang on tight.

It was the first real hug I'd received since my brother had died. I didn't tell her that, but in that moment, hugging her, comforting her... Death didn't look as bad anymore. The future didn't look as bleak. Because when she pulled back... when her eyes met mine, I saw hope.

EIGHTEEN

So I hug complete strangers and cry in their arms?
Tell me something I don't know!

Kiersten

He probably thought I was insane, but I couldn't pull back. Logically, my brain told me it was insane to feel so close to a guy I'd barely met. But emotionally? He'd picked up every little piece of emotional baggage I'd brought with me to college, unzipped it, and cleaned house.

Part of me was furious. But the other part of me? The one still holding onto Wes like he was my lifeline — just felt free. He did, in five minutes, what two years of therapy and endless amounts of antidepressants had failed to do. He'd helped me forgive. I knew it wasn't that easy; it couldn't be. Was it really just about thinking about the story differently? The odd thing was, everything he said about my parents was spot on. It was true. He made me believe the story because I knew for a fact that was how they were.

"Kiersten?" Wes murmured against my wet cheek. His

breath created a cooling sensation, causing me to shiver from my head to my toes, "You okay?"

I let out a heavy sigh. "Do you think I'm crazy?"

Wes laughed. "We're all a bit crazy; it's what makes us human."

I pushed against his chest.

"Wes?" a male voice said from behind me. I turned to see the guy that had been in the cafeteria that one day.

"David." Wes stood and helped me to my feet. "Everything all right?"

"Course." David cleared his throat and then dialed someone on his phone. "He's fine, sir. Yes, he was just out… running with a girl." David's smile fell. "Of course, sure I'll remind him, yes. Thank you, sir… Sorry, sir."

Wes released my hand and crossed his arms. "So, the general's orders?"

David shoved his phone in his pocket. "He just said to keep your priorities straight. Your health, football, school. And then friends."

Ouch! That made me last.

"Right." Wes nodded. "Thanks, David. I'll text you if I need you."

David stood his ground.

Something close to a low growl emerged from Wes's throat. "What? You're going to follow me now?"

"Orders." David sighed and shrugged. "I'm sorry, Wes. My job's at stake. You know how it is."

"I do," Wes muttered a vulgar curse under his breath and turned to me. "I'm sorry, Kiersten. I need to go. My father, it seems, is concerned about my priorities." His smile was tense.

"Can I see you tonight? Seems like we have some things we still gotta take care of."

"I don't know." I looked at David's disapproving glare and back at the ground. "I, uh, I think I'm busy."

Wes frowned in frustration.

"Come on, Wes." David reached for his arm.

"No." Wes didn't move. "Not until she says yes."

"Wes, just stop. Parents are important. If your father wants—"

"What he wants is two healthy sons," Wes said in an icy voice. "What he *has* is me. He'll take what he can get. I'll be at your dorm tonight at seven."

"Not tonight," I said. "But tomorrow's Friday. Date night, okay?"

"Okay." He swallowed, the color returning to his cheeks as his jaw seemed to relax. Why did he suddenly look so weak? "I'll see you then."

I watched Wes walk away, and I grew more curious by the second. Why did the quarterback of the football team look so pale all the time? And why, when he stepped into the shadows of the trees, did he lean on that David guy as if he was going to pass out? And if he was feeling sick, why the heck did he want to go running?

Thoughts plagued my mind as I made my way all the way back to the dorms. The last thing I wanted was to get close to a guy that made me feel as good as Wes did, only to have him ripped from my life because I wasn't high on his daddy's priority list.

Ugh.

I unlocked the door to our dorm and waltzed in.

"'Sup." Gabe waved and flipped through a few TV channels. "You can thank me later, you know."

"Thank you?"

"For the protein shake and banana waiting for consumption on the counter. I may have been bird watching and seen you walking down the path to the dorms."

"Bird watching?" I rolled my eyes. "And what birds were you watching, nature man?"

"The gray ones," Gabe answered, straight-faced.

"Pigeons?"

"Pigeons aren't gray."

"Are you colorblind?" I laughed and shook my head. "Okay, fine. So you were watching pigeons because why?"

Gabe threw the remote against the cushions on the couch and stood, raising his arms high above his head, revealing more tattoos on his hips trailing up his stomach. "I was worried."

"About the bird population?"

"You," Gabe growled. "I know you like him, I just…" He bit down on his lower lip. "Something about him worries me, and you are only a freshman."

"Thanks for the warning. Next time a girl jumps into your bed, I'll be sure to give her a heads up. You know, as a thank you for all your protectiveness."

Gabe shrugged and walked into the kitchen. "Pretty sure they all have to sign a release form anyway."

"Disgusting."

He laughed.

"So, where's my shake?"

"Here." He turned around and did a booty shake, then dropped it like it was hot in the kitchen.

I fell into fits of laughter before he turned back around and held up his finger while he fished out his phone, put on some music, and grabbed my hands.

Rocketship by Shane Harper came on. We danced in circles and then bumped hips.

Gabe released me and danced, really well, over to the cups above the sink and pulled one down, then continued dancing while he mixed banana with the protein shake.

He dipped his finger in it and licked, then did the same for me, holding out his finger for me to lick.

I shook my head no.

He leaned in and whispered, "Just one taste."

"Said the senior to the freshman."

"Once won't kill you."

"You're the guy drug officers warn teens about, aren't you? The one that says just one time won't get you addicted?"

Gabe smirked. "Why, Kiersten, are you afraid you're going to get addicted to me?"

"Fine." I licked the sugary substance off his finger.

"You like him a lot."

"What?" I stepped back and moved around him to grab my glass, but Gabe's arms came around my waist, twisting me around.

"I know girls." He shook his head and winced. "Believe me, I know them well, and nothing about me is causing you to falter. Absolutely nothing. I bet even if I kissed you, you'd be thinking about him. Shit, Kiersten, it's been four days! You're going to get your little heart broken if you fall for him, and then I'm going to have to pick up the pieces, and you'll probably sleep with me to feel better, wake up hating yourself and jump into a downward spiral of using men to fill the void *he* left in your life."

"Whoa."

"My point," he said, grabbing my wrists, "is that this can all be avoided. Just don't give him your everything — not until you know the return will be the same."

I shook away from his hold and took a long sip of my shake. "Why are you saying all this? You hardly know me."

Gabe snorted. "My point exactly. I don't know you. He doesn't know you. The only person that's going to fight for you right now is you. Don't let yourself lose sight of your biggest ally. Don't allow yourself to be blinded by pretty smiles and hot bodies — not even mine."

My eyebrows arched at his confidence.

"Don't get me wrong." Gabe held up his hands. "You're sexy as hell, but I would never shit where I like to stay."

"Huh?"

"It's a compliment." Gabe snickered. "You don't sleep with cousins' best friends, or roommates, or girls who don't know themselves yet. It's not fair. And in the end, it's just inviting heartbreak."

"You seem like you speak from experience." I tilted my head to get a better look at his piercing eyes.

Gabe swore and looked away. "I do. And that's all you need to know. She ruined me, Kiersten. And damn, if I wouldn't give my entire world to be ruined over and over again if it meant I could be a part of her universe."

I pushed him toward the main room and sat on the couch. "What happened?"

"Apparently, I'm the guy you date to piss your parents off. I'm the guy you date before a better offer, one involving multi-million-dollar business deals, comes bustling through."

I reached for his hand. "Gabe, I'm sorry."

"Don't be; it was years ago," he said with a shrug. "I'm an old soul and all that." Then he yawned again and slapped his leg, stood, and walked toward the door. "Remember our little chat." Glancing over his shoulder, he wrinkled his nose. "And take a shower; you smell like hell."

"Thanks." I rolled my eyes.

He paused at the door. "I could join you if you get lonely and need someone to wash your back."

I pointed to the door. "Bye, Gabe."

Laughing, he left.

Part of me hated that he was right. I could see myself doing exactly that, holding onto Wes as if he was my survival and then dying if, in the end, it didn't turn out the way I needed it to.

I couldn't lose myself in him. I refused to.

I chugged the rest of my protein shake and made my way into the bathroom.

NINETEEN

I'm not freaking out — not yet. Why hasn't she called back?

Weston

I knew I was being ridiculous when, during class, I kept checking my phone for any missed texts or phone calls Kiersten hadn't responded to me. And I hated that my mind was absolute crap while I made excuses for why she wouldn't talk to me.

Was it because of my dad?

Or did I push her too far, too fast?

Shit.

My phone vibrated in my hand. Finally!

I looked down at the text.

> We still on for 2night?

I was barely able to hide my excitement. As it was, I had such a giant-assed grin on my face that I'm sure my professor assumed I was high or looking at dirty pictures or something.

"Something you want to share with the rest of the class, Mr. Michels?" Crap, so she had noticed.

I cleared my throat and nodded. "I have a date."

A few people whispered around me.

And then I received a slap or two on the back from teammates. My professor, however, seemed less than amused. She rolled her eyes and returned to her lecture. But I couldn't concentrate. Instead, I texted her back.

Counting down the minutes.

So I'd lost every ounce of game I'd carefully pieced together throughout my existence. I didn't want to play the cool and aloof guy. The one that had all the time in the world, because I knew I didn't. And I wanted to capture every damn moment until it was too late.

My hands shook.

I checked my phone again.

I'd need to do another batch of meds before I saw her tonight. If I skipped my next class, took them about an hour early, and lay down, I'd probably be fine for the date. At least, fine enough not to puke all over her pretty face.

Ten minutes later, I strolled out of the room and made a beeline for the dorms.

TWENTY

Why hadn't I realized until now that I'd never been on a date? What do I wear? Are we eating? Holy crap! I think I'm going to be sick...

Kiersten

"**D**oes it look okay? Really?" I asked for the twentieth time.

Gabe smacked his hand against his forehead and cursed. "Just chill out! Geez, I have half a mind to give you alcohol right now. Sit. It's almost ready."

I smirked.

Another deadpan expression from Gabe as he ran the iron over the white shirt. "I take this to my grave, you know."

"What? The white shirt?" I asked innocently.

"No." He rolled his eyes and unplugged the iron. "My Martha Stewart skills."

"He can sew too," Lisa announced as she walked into the room and dangled a necklace in front of my face. "In fact, I'm pretty sure if you asked him to knit you a sweater, you'd have one by Christmas."

"Thanks, cousin." Gabe flipped her off and threw the shirt at me.

"Hey!" I caught it midair. "We don't want all your hard work going to waste."

"I need more guy friends," Gabe mumbled as he took a seat on the couch and sighed into his hands.

Lisa gasped. "I'm offended! You know I'm your favorite."

His eyes narrowed. "You know you're a loser when your best friend is your cousin."

"Aw, Gabe." Lisa pressed her hand to her chest. "That's the nicest thing you've ever said to me."

"Right." He folded his arms and groaned, leaning his head back on the couch. "I need a smoke."

"You quit," Lisa sang.

"Fine, then I need alcohol."

"You don't drink anymore."

I laughed when Gabe gave me an exasperated look. He pushed to his feet and walked over to the kitchen. I heard water running and then cursing.

"Don't mind him." Lisa waved in Gabe's direction. "He really isn't as annoyed as he seems. Promise."

"Lies," he yelled from the kitchen.

"Now…" Lisa pointed to my t-shirt. "Strip. He worked hard on this, and I want to make sure it looks good with the skirt."

"Uh…" I shook my head no. "Gabe's in the kitchen, like right there. I'll change in my room."

"It's like he's gay. I promise he won't notice." Lisa nodded emphatically. Another curse was heard from the kitchen. Poor Gabe.

"Fine." I quickly took off my T-shirt and reached for the

one she held out to me. I slowly did the buttons and then stood for her to examine me. I had a cute miniskirt with tan and white stripes that hugged every curve and a white button-up blouse that hung loosely over my hips. In my mind, I thought it would look awful, but by the large smile on Lisa's face, I could tell I was the one in the wrong.

"Damn," Gabe said from behind me.

I jerked around.

He grinned. "Oh, and by the way, not gay and most definitely watched." He said *watched* with such a predatory snap of his teeth that I took a step back.

"Gabe, stop scaring her," Lisa scolded. "Now, Kiersten, put on the necklace and heels, and you'll be ready."

I did as she said and then stood in front of both of them and did a quick turn.

Gabe leaned forward, his forearms flexing against his legs as he put pressure on his legs to stand. "Nope. Change."

"What? Why?" I felt my face fall. "Doesn't it look good?"

"Lisa, do you want her to be taken advantage of?" He shook his head and walked around me like a tiger stalking its prey.

"The top isn't even low! She has it buttoned for crying out loud!" Lisa argued.

"Right," Gabe snarled.

Before I knew what was happening, he'd reached around me and put two of his fingers directly on my chest at the last button. "And every damn minute of the night he's going to wonder how many seconds it will take to strip every last button on her shirt."

"The skirt's fine." Lisa stood her ground.

"Right." Gabe's hand moved to my skirt and gave it a little tug. "It may as well be a second skin the way it hugs every single curve, and you know what guys think."

Lisa rolled her eyes. I, however, stood frozen in place.

"He's going to want to touch her legs. He's going to want to—"

"Gabe!" Lisa stood to her feet and marched over to us. "Is this about him? Or you?"

"I don't want in her pants!" he all but yelled.

"Um, I'm standing right here," I said in a quiet voice.

Gabe paced around the room in front of me. "It's about him. What if he touches her? What if she can't find her whistle, and—"

"You're going to be *such* a great dad," Lisa announced. "Now, it's time to cut the apron strings. Tell her she looks pretty and let it go."

Gabe crossed his arms and pouted.

I waited with Lisa.

Finally, he swore and looked me in the eyes. "You look really pretty."

"Thank you!" I slowly walked over to him and kissed him on the cheek. "That means a lot."

"Lisa," Gabe said with gravel in his voice. "Give us a minute."

"But—"

"I said, give us a minute."

"Fine." She stomped off into her room, leaving me alone with Gabe.

"Do you know how to hit a guy?" he asked, grabbing my hands. "If I pull you close to my body, do you know how to knee me, where to knee me?"

I lifted my knee quickly, causing Gabe to stumble back and smile. "Well done."

"Anything else, Dad?" I laughed.

He growled and pulled me close again. "If he tries to touch you, if he does anything that you don't want, you blow the damn whistle and call me. I don't care what time of night it is, okay?"

I sighed and nodded.

Gabe released me.

"Why are you so protective of me? You don't even know me." I went to sit on the couch, waiting for Wes to come pick me up.

"No freaking clue." Gabe took a seat next to me and put his arm around the back of the couch. "I just can't stand the idea of something happening to you. And even though I keep saying this until I'm blue in the face, it's not because I'm jealous. I just… I have a really bad feeling about him."

"You gotta let the baby birds fly, Gabe." I smacked his knee. "And you have to trust my judgment. He's been a complete gentleman with me."

"I know that." Gabe pinched the bridge of his nose. "But don't you think it's weird? His entourage? The fact that he's an RA? I mean, why is he an RA? I even asked a few of the other upperclassmen. It was never supposed to be him, and nobody's talking. And then the whole football thing. One of my friends on the team said he collapsed at practice. What if he's on drugs or something?"

"I highly doubt that." I shook my head, refusing to believe it. "I think he's probably just overwhelmed. I mean, wouldn't you be?"

After a while, Gabe answered. "Probably. Just be careful."

"And for the twentieth time," I sang out. "I will."

At the sound of the knock on the door, my heart began

thumping against my chest as if it was going to beat its way out and land on the floor.

Lisa ran from her room, nearly tripping over the table blocking her way, and stopped in front of the door, fixed her hair, and swung open the door.

TWENTY-ONE

For the first time in a year, I wanted to live — because I wanted to spend every freaking day watching her open her eyes to the world. Hell, I wanted to be the first thing she saw. Sometimes, reality's a bitch.

Weston

I don't know what I'd thought she'd be wearing — but it wasn't that. It was a short skirt, a billowy shirt, and high heels made to make guys want to touch her feet. And I was so not a foot person.

"You look…" I swallowed. "Beautiful."

I heard Gabe grunt behind her. So clearly, he still wasn't a fan. I made a mental note to try to win him over later that week rather than sit by and listen to him grunt and groan every time I paid a compliment to the girl I liked.

Aw, crap. I was crushing. And I really didn't have the luxury of doing that. I looked at her skirt again and the legs that led up to those full cute hips. Damn.

"You ready?" I croaked, sounding like a pubescent teen.

"Sure." She smiled warmly and grabbed a strappy thing I can only assume was a purse, either that or a weapon. I held out my arm and escorted her out the door.

"Got your whistle?" I asked.

"Check."

"Cell phone?"

"Check."

"List?"

She stopped walking and looked up into my eyes. "You know you really don't have to help me with that. I mean, I'm sure I can—"

"Stop." I pressed a finger to her lips. "We're going to tackle the list, but remember, I said I could only help with a few. That whole falling in love thing will have to be saved for someone who's worthy of that heart of yours."

She laughed. "How do you know my heart's good?"

I stopped and pressed my palm flat against her chest, relishing the way her healthy heart slammed against my skin. I could almost feel it beating for my heart, making it stronger. I pulled back, noticing the flush in her cheeks.

"It's a good heart. Strong beat, though I'm pretty sure it skipped one when I touched you."

"Very funny." She looked away.

"I can tell you have a good heart…" I sighed, opening the door to the outside. "…because the minute I met you, I wanted to fight for it."

She was silent.

"That's how you can tell when someone has a good heart."

"When you want to start a war?" She laughed, clearly trying to lighten my mood.

"Nah." I sighed. "When you want to be the one to make it beat."

I seriously needed to stop coming on so strong. I was going

to send her screaming down the street, and I really didn't want to see her sprain her ankle in those kick-ass heels.

"This is me." I pointed to the black Porsche Cayenne and opened her door for her. It was the only car I owned that wasn't so exotic people wanted to stab me in the eye. I'd wanted a truck for my sixteenth birthday. My dad had gotten me a Mercedes that politicians drove, complete with bullet-proof glass. The Cayenne was my purchase, the first day I was able to access my trust fund.

Kiersten was quiet. I quickly ran over to my side and jumped into the SUV.

Kiersten's hands ran down the leather seats, her eyes taking in every single detail of the interior. Funny how years ago I would have never done that, but now? Now I got it. Because you never knew when a moment would be your last. So why not soak up every last memory? Like now, the sun was just starting to go down, which meant part of it was shining into the car directly across her red hair, making it appear like it was glowing.

I sighed.

She turned to look at me. "What are you doing?"

"Staring," I answered honestly. "I think you owe me that, especially since you felt me up the first time we met."

She hid her face in her hands. "I did not!" Her cute voice was muffled by her hands, still covering her face.

"Um, you did." I started the car. "I'll take it to my grave, don't worry." Shit, I really needed to stop with those comments.

I checked my watch; hopefully, I-5 wasn't a complete mess. I really didn't want to miss our first stop.

"So?" She fidgeted with her seatbelt. "Where are we going?"

"Bungee jumping," I answered with a deadpan expression.

"It is on your list, isn't it?"

Her eyes widened as she looked down at her skirt then back up at me.

"I won't look. Promise."

She swatted me across the stomach.

"Fine, fine." I laughed. "Just don't hit me. We're going on a date."

"I know that."

"Then…" I took the first exit. "That's really all you need to know, isn't it?"

It had been years since I'd actually taken a girl out. With football practice and the fact that Lorelei refused to go anywhere in public unless it was some sort of celebrity event, it had been a while.

"Almost there." I took the next left and drove down the private road. I knew she probably didn't have any idea where we were, which kind of excited me. I didn't want her to freak though. "Still got your whistle?"

"Why?" Her eyes darted to mine. "Am I going to need it?"

"No." I laughed. "Just checking."

"Are you taking me into the woods to kill me?"

"Um, no."

She exhaled.

"If I was going to kill you, I probably wouldn't make it known that we were out on a date at all. Pretty sure Gabe would come running around the corner, guns blazing the minute you didn't text them to say you were okay."

Kiersten laughed. "That's true, I guess."

I loved her laugh. I was turning into a lunatic — a craving, needing, drug-addicted insane person. I put the car in park and turned it off.

"What are we—"

"Get out of the car," I said nicely. "And I'll show you."

We were at Lake Washington, in a private, secluded spot owned by my family. No interruptions and nothing crazy. Just us. Thank God. I even told James and David that if they showed up, I'd find a way to get them fired.

Pissed, they'd finally given up when I told them they could at least track my movements and my vitals through the freaky doctor technology given to us by my dad's so-called experts.

"So, now what?" Kiersten crossed her arms and looked out at the lake. She seemed nervous. Her eyes kept darting from the water down to the rocky ground as if she wasn't really sure where to look. Apparently, anywhere but at me.

"One," I said.

"What?" Her head snapped up.

"One." I reached for her hands and pulled her against my chest. "We can cross off number one on the list."

Her brow furrowed, and then realization kicked in, and her eyes widened. "Oh, no! I mean, we already kissed, we did that. I—"

"Shh." I bit down on my lip, telling myself to take my time tasting her. This wasn't to prove a point. This was me showing her what it was like to be truly kissed. "If I remember correctly, your list said 'kiss a hot guy.'"

"Yeah, but—"

"I'm changing it. You see, all guys want to be kissed by a girl. But you? You deserve to be the one receiving the kiss, not giving. That's not how this works. So I'm deeming myself the hot guy, and I'm going to kiss you. I'm going to kiss you so hard that you forget everything but my lips pressed against yours." I brushed some of her lush red hair away from her face and tapped my fingertips against her jaw as they ran up the side of her cheek and lightly tugged her head forward. "I'm going to taste you like you deserve to be tasted."

Her lower lip trembled.

"I'm going to make it so hard for you to forget this first kiss that you don't want anyone else kissing you ever again. When the guy you fall in love with kisses you — it better put this kiss to shame — if it doesn't, then he isn't the right guy. Because I'm going to do a damn good job, and I want the guy that earns you, that takes that heart of yours and holds it in the palm of his hands… I want that guy to be able to make you feel things I'll just be tapping into. Do you understand, Kiersten?"

My voice was hoarse. I hadn't meant to say all that. I hadn't meant to turn it into a goodbye kiss before we'd really said hello. But that was what it felt like because I realized in that moment. I probably wasn't going to be that guy. I'd be cold, dead, in the ground, and she'd be warm and alive. I swallowed and touched my fingertips to her lips. "I want the earth to shift."

My hands moved to the side of her neck, and I caressed her smooth skin and tugged her even closer to my lips until our mouths were a breath apart. "So this is me…" I kissed her softly across the mouth, massaging her lower lip with mine, forming it, not pushing it, so that when she responded, she knew the exact pressure it would take for the kiss to be sealed. "A hot boy…" I smiled against her mouth. "…trying to kiss, a very pretty, very beautiful, very deserving girl." My hand slipped to her chest, not to feel her up, but to touch what I so craved. Her heart beat wildly against my hand. "This is me, taking the very first thing off your list. And now I'm going to stop talking…"

Her breath hitched as my mouth met hers in such a whisper that it was almost as if we weren't touching, but we were. Her lips were wet. I licked along the seam, breaking them apart and then slowly letting her taste take over. I pushed my tongue against the inside of her mouth, loving the way her body tensed as the pressure increased.

She moaned, putting her arms around my neck. I helped her, rocking her harder against my body. My hands came around her back, and I tried to get all of her to press against me. I'd never felt so alive as when that girl, that perfectly strange girl who I'd only met days before, was near me. I could almost believe her heartbeat was my own as her tongue danced with mine. I increased the pressure, cupping her chin with my hand. I moved my lips down her neck and behind her ear. Alternating between trailing hot kisses down her neck and blowing against the coolness my kisses left when my lips released their hold. Damn, I wanted to bite her. I wanted to keep tasting her over and over again until I had no strength left, but that was just the thing. Always a time limit, always a buzzer when it came to me.

We broke apart slowly, both of our chests heaving.

She opened her mouth, but I pressed my fingers against it.

"Ready for the next part of your date?" I didn't want her to discuss the kiss like most girls would or feel awkward about it. So I just changed the subject. Mainly because I didn't want her to embarrass herself, and also because I was feeling a hell of a lot of arousal in my body, and I didn't want to draw attention to myself. My self-control was that of a thirteen-year-old boy.

It took everything in me not to be selfish and throw her against my car, lifting that tiny skirt until my hands—

Right.

I shook my head. Clearly, the kiss had affected me. I wanted it to be romantic for her. I told her I wanted her world to change. Hadn't expected mine to shift as well.

"The other part of the date?" She grinned. Her face was flushed. "You mean you didn't just take me out here to make out?"

"Yes." I grinned. "No." Cursing, I ran my hands through my hair. "Okay, guilty on both accounts. Fine. To be fair, I wish I could kiss you all damn night, but kissing always leads to…"

"Hugging?" She gave me a saucy wink.

"Right." I laughed and looked away. "Lots of tight, uh, hugging."

"So…" She looked back at the car. "Do we get in or what?"

"Nope." I reached into my pocket and pulled out a blindfold. "Now, you trust me."

"Should have known you'd wait until after you kissed me to kill me."

"All the good serial killers seduce and then kill." I sighed. "Now, give me two minutes to set up, and we'll be ready to go."

"Okay."

I waved in front of her face to make sure she couldn't see and then ran back to the Cayenne.

TWENTY-TWO

He was right. My world shifted.
It shifted into his atmosphere. I wonder if it was on purpose.

Kiersten

Why did people always do that? Wave in front of your face to make sure you couldn't see? I mean, I could still see the action of him waving. It was cute. And honestly, I needed a moment. After that kiss… I sighed and rocked back on my heels. His kisses didn't give — they ruined. I wasn't sure how any other kiss would ever compare. But I did know one thing. I didn't want to experiment. I didn't want to see. Yet it felt like he was just humoring me because, in those moments, he always said "the guy who holds your heart," and "the guy you marry…" Why the heck was he constantly taking himself out of the equation? The insecure part of myself made me assume it was because I wasn't his type, and I was young. And well, he was a popular football god, while I was just a freshman with an undeclared major. Wow, there was a reality check if I ever needed one.

"Ready?" His voice came from in front of me.

"I think so." I tried not to sound nervous, but I was. I mean, if he kissed me again, I might just pass out and fall into the lake. Hopefully, he knew how to swim because I was probably going to drown.

"Open up your hands."

"Please don't be one of those guys that thinks it's funny to put spiders or snakes in girls' hands to hear them scream."

A warm hand touched my face and then flicked my lower lip. "I can't lie, Kiersten. I want to hear you scream, but not like that. Definitely, not like that."

Was he saying what I thought he was saying? Regardless, I felt a hot blush rush across my cheeks.

"You trust me?" Wes asked.

"Yes."

"Then hold out your hands."

I did.

He placed something kind of heavy in them. It was wrapped, so I couldn't tell by feeling it what it was. A book maybe?

The blindfold was pulled from my face. I looked down at my hands. It was a book. At least, I think it was.

"Open it," he urged.

As I peeled back the layers of blue wrapping paper, Wes walked behind me and whispered in my ear.

"…It was painful, exceedingly painful, to know that they were under obligations to a person who could never receive a return…"

The paper fell. It was a limited edition of Pride and Prejudice. "You, you gave me—"

"Mr. Darcy," Wes whispered in my ear. "As you can see, I also memorized some lines so that you'd swoon."

"Should you recite them again, and I'll fall into your arms?" I asked breathlessly, still examining the beautifully bound book.

"It would help my pride." He nipped my ear with his lips, and then his hands moved to my neck, massaging my shoulders. "But then again, it is called *Pride and Prejudice* for a reason."

I turned in his arms and hugged him. "Thank you so much."

"Best first date gift you've ever received?" he asked, pulling away.

"It's the only first date gift I've had, so sure." I giggled.

"Damn." He tilted my chin and gazed into my eyes. "I'll just have to do better."

"Memorize the entire book, and we'll talk."

"Really?" His mouth curved into a wicked smile. "You do know that I was a child prodigy, right? With the piano? And music? As in, my father almost made me do music instead of football? Photographic memory. So don't go challenging me to memorize Jane Austen; I may just get bored enough to do it."

I laughed and hugged him again. I loved the way he smelled, the way he felt against my skin. I didn't want to ever think about him graduating. It made me sick.

"And on to the rest of the date." He grabbed my hand and led me back to the car. "You ready?"

"Sure." I put the book on my lap, careful not to let it fall, and watched in disappointment as we made our way back to the school.

I was ready to jump out my own window when we pulled up to my dorm, and Wes escorted me to the door. Had he changed his mind? Embarrassed, I told myself it was silly to feel so rejected, especially after everything he'd done. It was ridiculous! It wasn't as if we were dating!

"So…" He braced my shoulders with his hands. "Your list said to make two real friends. Well, honestly, I think you have three right underneath your nose without even knowing it. Damn," he said, shaking his head. "I'm good at this list thing."

I laughed out loud just as the door opened, revealing Gabe and Lisa. Lisa giggled and held open her arms. "Welcome to the rest of your date!"

"You knew?" I hugged my book to my chest and smiled.

"Of course!" Lisa pulled my arm, tugging me into the main room. "I didn't fill Gabe in until after you left, though thus his haggard appearance."

I gave Gabe a pitiful smile as he rolled his eyes from the couch. He still hadn't changed out of his jeans and white t-shirt, whereas Lisa was wearing a killer dress.

"Okay, it's time!" She clapped her hands and disappeared into the kitchen.

"So it's like a double date?" I elbowed Wes, who laughed and shot Gabe a humored look.

"Laugh it up guys." Gabe cursed. "Why is it that I get a date with my cousin, and you get her?" He pointed at me while he was talking to Wes.

"Just lucky, I guess," Wes answered.

"True." Gabe winked in my direction. "Well, the good news is I don't have to kill you." He was talking to Wes again. "She seems unharmed."

"Except for the kiss," I said with as much seriousness as I could.

Gabe's eyebrows arched as he examined me and then slowly turned to Wes.

"Thanks." Wes nodded in my direction. "Throwing me under the bus for doing you a favor, nice."

I smirked.

"It was on her list," Wes explained. "One I'm helping her with."

"You were on her list?"

"Ah…" I stepped between them and set my book down on the table, careful not to drop it too hard. "I believe I wrote, 'kiss a hot guy.'"

"Hi." Wes held out his hand. "Hot guy. Now, what's that make you?"

Gabe shook his head and then burst out laughing. "Clearly not hot, but she did call me nice yesterday."

"Ouch." Wes winced.

"Right. It's like cutting off a dog's balls without putting him to sleep first. She didn't even give me a warning, just a 'hey, you're nice.'"

"Still recovering?" Wes asked.

"I may whore around later this week to prove a point." Gabe gave a haphazard shrug. "We'll see."

"Men are animals," Lisa said, coming back into the main room. "All right, I've got chocolate, fruity drinks, and the movie. Anything else?"

"I think we're good." Wes wrapped his arm around me and pulled me close. I noticed Gabe watching us, but it wasn't with jealousy. It was more like concern, which in turn made me want to feel concerned too.

Wes stumbled a bit as we made our way to the couch.

"Hey." I steadied him. "You okay?"

"Fine." But he was pale again. "I just… can I use your bathroom?"

"Sure," Lisa spoke up. "You can go through either one of our rooms. We share a bathroom, so it doesn't matter."

"Cool, thanks." He got up from the couch, still unsteady on his feet, and made his way to my room.

"He okay?" Lisa asked me.

"I'm sure he's just tired," I lied. Curious myself as to why a six-five, perfectly healthy quarterback would suddenly look like he'd been drinking all night long.

"Be right back." Gabe shot up from his seat and went the same direction Wes had.

"Uh-oh," Lisa murmured. "That can't be good."

TWENTY-THREE

Time was running out fast. I could feel it from the tingling in my hands to the erratic beating of my heart—why was I suddenly finding it so damn hard to realize the end was near? Probably because she made me feel new—like a new beginning.

Weston

I gripped the counter and told myself to keep all the contents of my stomach in instead of out.

My cell rang.

David.

I pressed ignore and started my typical breathing exercises. It wasn't healthy for me to panic. In and out, in and out. I held my breath and chanced another look in the mirror.

My phone went off again. This time it was James.

Time for your next set of meds.

Right, like I wanted to take more pills that made me feel shittier and quite possibly would ruin my date.

I'm fine.

I texted back and slipped the phone into my pocket.

I flexed my arms as I braced the counter and breathed in and out through my nose as the nausea came and went. I couldn't go on like this. The last set of drugs before Christmas were supposed to be the strongest, the doctor's final hat trick, only I was worried they were hurting more than helping. If I had to keep taking them, I wouldn't be able to play football. I wouldn't be able to run. I wouldn't be able to live. I'd be lying in bed sick as a dog as the days ran into each other until finally, I just didn't wake up.

"Hey." The door pushed open. Gabe walked himself right in and shut the door behind him. "What the hell are you doing?"

"Not the time, Gabe."

"The hell it isn't!" He grabbed me by the shirt, not a smart move considering I had at least five inches on him, but whatever. I was too weak to care. "What the hell are you taking? Oxy? Meth?"

I laughed. Not because it was funny, but because, for a second, I wished it was a drug problem. Damn, how pathetic was that?

"No." I bit down on my lip. The nausea was finally passing, the feeling returning to my extremities. "Nothing like that."

"You better not be messing with her." Gabe released me and hit the door with his hand. "I swear I'll kill you if you hurt her."

"I just want to be her friend. Honest." I lied. I wanted more. But people didn't always get what they wanted.

The nausea came back full force, causing me to double over in pain as, I swear, knives started attacking my stomach. "Hold on, give me a second."

"Dude." Gabe put his hand on my back. "What's wrong? You got the flu or something?"

"Or something," I said through clenched teeth. "I'm fine; I just get… episodes." It was the best I could do without lying.

"Like nervous episodes?" Gabe asked.

"Yeah, like that."

"Sorry." He swore. "I just… that girl is important, okay? Don't ask me how or why I know she is; I just know. There's something about her. She's frail, and I don't want you messing with her just because she's a hot piece of ass, okay?"

"I swear…" It hurt like hell, but I stood to my full height. "…that I'm not messing with her. I want to help, and I want to be her friend."

"Friends don't kiss."

I forced a laugh. "You sound like her."

Gabe didn't join in the laughter. Great, I'd pissed him off again.

"Look." I crossed my arms and tried to concentrate on anything but the pain in my chest and stomach. "I like that girl. I won't hurt her. Hell, I won't even touch her again. I'm not going to steal her virginity. I'm not going to make her promises I can't keep."

"How do I know I can believe you?"

"Tell you what." I put my arm around his and opened the door. "Why don't you just trust me, and if I do something that royally pisses you off or I screw up, you can beat the shit out of me. Deal?"

Gabe was silent, and then he held out his hand. "It will be a pleasure kicking your ass."

"Too bad you won't get the chance." I shook his hand just as Lisa walked through the door.

"Uh, everything okay?"

"Perfect." Gabe's grip tightened against mine. "We were just talking sports."

Lisa snorted. "Fine. Can we start the movie?"

"Sure thing." I released Gabe's hand. He gave me a swift nod.

When we made our way back into the room, Lisa was sitting on one end of the couch, and Gabe maneuvered next to her, leaving just the love seat for me and Kiersten. At least the night was going to end on a good note.

Lisa pressed play.

"Wait!" I yelled, holding up my hand. I grabbed the drinks Lisa had brought in and pulled a tiny paper umbrella from my pocket. Grinning, I dropped it onto the side of Kiersten's drink. "A fruity drink with an umbrella."

"You got any more of those in there?" Lisa asked.

I laughed, finally feeling more relaxed now that the date was well on its way and Kiersten knew my plan. "Sure." With a tug, I had about five different colored umbrellas set out on the coffee table. "Okay, now we can start the movie."

"Thank you." Kiersten's lips grazed my ear, making me horny as hell during the opening credits. "For my best first date ever, my umbrella, my kiss, and my book. The way you're blowing through the list, we won't have much to do in a week."

My stomach clenched.

Hell, no.

What was I thinking?

I needed to go slower.

I shrugged and whispered back, "Well, the other tasks are a lot harder. It may take a while."

"Fine by me." She reached for my hand and didn't let go.

I looked up.

Gabe was watching us intently, his eyes narrowing as he looked at her hand then back at my face. I felt stuck. I wanted to date her. In a normal situation, I would have flipped him off and thrown her into my bedroom without a second thought.

But now?

I wanted to treasure the feeling of her fingertips against mine because I was pretty sure in a few months… I wouldn't have that luxury.

TWENTY-FOUR

I hate how much I like him. Almost as much as I hate it when I'm not able to be with him all the time. I am falling way too hard and fast. Someone catch me, stop me, call me crazy, slap me — geez, just don't let me get my hopes up.

Kiersten

It was officially two months since I met Wes. Ever since our first date, I'd seen him almost every day for lunch and at least twice a week for movie nights at our place.

Basically, he was everywhere. A permanent fixture in my life. So regular, in fact, that people no longer stared; they just seemed to expect it.

The only thing I couldn't put my finger on was the fact that he was losing weight. I mean, he still looked hot, but his muscles seemed more defined, his jaw even sharper than before. When I mentioned it, he just laughed off my concern and said practices were hell.

"So what chapter we on?" Wes dropped his lunch onto our regular table and took a swig of water.

I grinned. "Last one."

"No way!" He pulled me in for a hug. "Killer job, it only took us over fifty days to finish one book."

"You know what that means?" I bit down on my lip and moved closer to him, scraping my chair against the floor.

"What?" He leaned in and flicked part of my hair. Good Lord, the boy was obsessed with hair, or maybe it was just with red. I didn't know which, but he was always touching it as if somehow my hair was going to fall out or disappear.

I swatted his hand away. "Just means we need another book when we finish. I'm thinking Mansfield Park or..." My voice trailed off. His face turned pale as he broke eye contact and fidgeted with his food.

"What?" He licked his lips and spread his salad around his plate like he wasn't sure if he wanted to eat it or just torture it.

"We don't have to read anymore. I mean, I know you have other friends, and it has been every lunch and—"

"Stop." He rolled his eyes and gave me that sexy grin I was so used to. "I was just upset about Mansfield Park. I don't really like that story. How about you pick something else, and we'll get started in on it after Thanksgiving break?"

"Okay." I smiled when he looked at me, but it was hollow. I could feel that it didn't reach my eyes. "Are you okay?"

"Of course," he said, almost too fast as he gave me another fake grin and cleared his throat. "Just got a lot of work to do before break, you know?"

"Oh." I tried not to sound disappointed. "Right, yeah, I have a lot of homework too."

"Between that and practice..." A shadow fell over his face. "I don't know. You know how you have rough days?"

"Yeah." I reached out and placed my hand on his arm. "We all do. It's good to know you're not perfect."

"So far from it." He reached for my hand and kissed it. "I uh, do sort of have a favor to ask you though."

"Okay." I shifted in my seat, suddenly nervous that he was going to ask me to not see him again or do something crazy and start dating, which actually wouldn't be the first time he'd suggested it. A month ago, he jokingly encouraged me to go on a date. I'd slammed the door in his face, and he spent the afternoon apologizing. So right, I overreacted, but it hurt my feelings. I mean, guys weren't that dense, were they? Couldn't he tell I liked him? As in, a lot more than he liked me?

I clenched my hands tightly in my lap and waited for the inevitable.

"Will you spend Thanksgiving break with me and my dad?"

So not what I was expecting.

"Huh?"

"Nothing, never mind." He reached for his tray and started to stand, but I grabbed his wrist.

"Wes, I'm not saying no; I just didn't expect that."

"Yeah?" His hands were shaking; either he was nervous or coming down with something. "What were you expecting?"

"Oh, you know… for you to try to set me up on another date and hurt my feelings."

Wes laughed loudly, earning the attention of people around the cafeteria. "Right. I think I learned my lesson last time, don't you?"

I shrugged.

"Shit." He let out a heavy sigh and grabbed my hand. "You know I like you, I just—"

"—don't date freshman." I cleared my throat nervously.

"And don't want Gabe to kick my ass."

"Please!" I rolled my eyes. "Like he could kick your ass."

His eyes clouded over before he gave me another heart-stopping smile. "I'll tell you what." He leaned in. "We'll date."

"What?"

"For two weeks." He grinned and held up two fingers. "For two weeks you're mine. We'll date, we'll hold hands — more than we do now." He brushed his thumb over my knuckles as he searched my eyes. "And at the end of two weeks, you'll realize I'm not as cool as you think I am and move on to greener pastures."

I felt my eyes narrow. "Is there a catch?"

"Of course." He laughed and tightened his grip on my hand as he leaned in. "You have to come home with me for the first week. That's Thanksgiving break, and then..." He stood, pushing his chair away from the table and got down on both knees. "And then you have to promise to be my date for Homecoming."

My mouth dropped open.

Was Weston Michels — football god — celebrity — holy hunk of hotness — on his knees in front of me asking me, not only to meet his dad but to go to Homecoming?

"Kind of uncomfortable down here."

I laughed and helped him to his feet, throwing my arms around his neck. "Yes! Yes! Yes!"

"Wait, is that a yes?" Wes swung me around the room and then did something so out of character I almost missed it.

He kissed me as if we really were dating.

He hadn't touched me since the first date we went on.

His lips brushed mine briefly and then harder as he set me on my feet and wrapped his arms around my waist. With little effort, he lifted me onto the table and cupped my face. "Thank you."

"For what?" I said breathlessly.

"Saying yes." He was totally serious. His face had that same shadow as before.

I touched his smooth jaw with my fingertips. "You really are having a rough day, aren't you?"

He clenched his teeth and gave a jerky nod.

Without thinking, I slid my arms around his neck and held him as tight as I could. "I think the star quarterback is allowed to have rough days, as long as..." I let my voice trail off.

"As long as what?" he said, taking the bait and pulling back, so our lips were really close again.

"As long as he promises to always share them with that nerdy freshman he keeps hanging out with."

"Not nerdy." He kissed my mouth. "Beautiful." And kissed me again. "Sexy." And again. "Gorgeous hair—"

"What is it with you and hair?" I laughed against his neck as he interlaced his fingers with mine.

"It's precious." He shrugged, helping me off the table. "That's all."

"Hair and hearts," I murmured. "Weird obsessions, but okay. I'll allow you some quirkiness on behalf of your hotness factor."

"How very gracious of you." He chuckled, kissing my hand. "Now, let's eat before you go to your next class. And then packing. I've got a freshman to take home for the week."

Yeah, I was probably never going to lose the smile on my face. Ever.

TWENTY-FIVE

Yeah, Gabe was going to murder me in my sleep.

Weston

I checked my phone. An hour had gone by. I'd figured Gabe would have stopped by my room already to yell or throw things or punch me in the face.

I expected him to at least send me a nasty text message about not keeping my promise.

A knock sounded on my door. Smiling, I opened it expecting to see a large fist flying toward my jaw. Instead, it was David and James.

Ugh. I'd rather be punched.

"How is your day progressing?" James asked, sounding oh–so-mechanical and ridiculous.

"Fantastic. I've got a date for Homecoming." I sat on my bed and glared.

"Do you normally have trouble getting dates?" David laughed.

"No." I scowled. "This girl's special."

James shifted on his feet. "Not to bring up a sore subject—"

"Then don't bring it up," I snapped.

"—But," James continued. "Do you think it's a smart move to get a girl involved in your life at this point? You've refused to take any tests until the day of your surgery. You have no idea what is going on in your body, and you want to involve someone as innocent as that girl?"

"Look—" I swear my teeth were gnashing together. "It's not your business. So stay out of it."

"It is my business." James tilted his head. "I'm your shrink. Your father hired me to look after your well-being."

"My father hired you because he doesn't want me to lose my shit and commit suicide like my brother. You aren't my surgeon, and you sure as hell aren't my friend. I'll do what I want — with or without your permission."

David heaved a sigh. "Wes—"

"Do you need anything else?" I interrupted.

With a curse, David pulled out his notebook. "I just need to document how you're feeling today. You know the drill. You get the drugs that cost a fortune and haven't been tested by the FDA yet, and we have to write it down. I don't do this to torture you. I'm not your doctor, I *am* your friend, and I've been your bodyguard since you threw your first football, so for the love of God, just tell me how you feel."

I felt guilty as hell. David was right. He'd been there through it all. It was the only way I could even stand having James around. David was family to me, and I was treating him like shit.

"I'm sorry," I murmured, my voice hoarse with too much emotion. I let out a sigh and began talking about my symptoms.

"I'm losing feeling in my right leg. I'm not sure if it's because I keep getting tackled or if it's the medicine. I throw up almost every morning, my chest doesn't hurt as much as it used to, and the nightmares have started to slowly go away. I'm not feeling depressed, just anxious like God has this giant ass timer in his hands and is just waiting to hit *end*."

"Very good." James cleared his throat and pressed stop on his recorder. Hadn't known he was recording but whatever.

David reached across the space between us and touched my arm. "Thank you, Wes. We'll leave you to your packing. You sure you still want to drive yourself?"

"Yup." I grinned, remembering Kiersten and her excitement. "I'm bringing my girlfriend."

James sighed heavily, but David grinned and said, "Good for you."

"Thanks."

They left the room, and I was emotionally ready to throw a bat at anything that talked to me.

"Hey, those goons bothering you?" Gabe said, launching himself into my room just as David and James left.

"Always." I groaned. "So please, punch me, get it over with."

Gabe looked guilty.

Oh no.

"Are you sick?" He asked in a quiet voice.

"How much did you hear?" I didn't look at him. I couldn't; if I did, I'd probably lose it and then just want to punch myself for crying like a baby.

"I know one's a shrink, and the other says you're on some sort of drugs that make you sick, and then I heard something about surgery."

A few seconds went by. Hell, I hadn't told anyone. I didn't want anyone to know because I wanted to feel normal if it was my last autumn on this earth.

"Yeah, man." I bit down on my lip, still refusing to make eye contact. "I'm sick."

"How sick?" Gabe sat in the chair by my desk. I could see his feet tapping against the floor; whether it was in nervousness or just awkwardness, I couldn't tell because I was still being a pansy and staring at the floor.

"Really sick." My voice broke. Damn it.

"Are you going to get better?"

I laughed without humor and finally lifted my gaze to meet his. "I have no idea. I find out in four weeks."

"What happens in four weeks?"

"Nosy bastard, aren't you?"

He grinned and gave me a haphazard shrug.

I sighed and shook my head. "Surgery, and if it doesn't work, or if I die during it, yeah, well… it's curtains, I guess on either end."

"So it's going to be fine then? You'll be fine?"

"Define 'fine'?" I laughed, the sound harsh in my quiet room. "If dying is fine, then yeah, I'll be fine. If living for a few more months while my body gets slowly stolen away from me by unhealthy cells, then yup. Fine, fine, fine, so damn, fine." I wiped my face with my hands and groaned.

"She doesn't know, does she?" Gabe asked.

"Hell, no."

"Don't tell her."

"What?" My head snapped up. "Are you sure that's a good idea?"

"It will only freak her out, especially since you're going to be fine, right?" He gave me a confident smile. "You can beat it."

It was the first time someone had said that to me.

Everyone else had been so concerned. David about the symptoms, my dad about depression, nobody — not even the doctor — had told me I was strong enough to take it.

I nodded jerkily, trying not to cry like a baby, and said, "You're right. I will beat it."

"Or I'll beat you." Gabe laughed. "For not only breaking her heart but dying after Homecoming. I mean, seriously? Even you have to admit how messed up that is."

"Yeah, well." I kicked off my shoes and lay down on the bed. "I like her. I want to spend time with her, and time isn't something I really have. It's a luxury, you know? People don't realize how lucky they are. Do you even realize how much it pisses me off when people complain about silly things like their lunch being crappy or their coffee tasting bad? I would drink shitty coffee and eat rotten food for the rest of my life if I could just *have* a life. You know?"

"Yeah," Gabe said softly. "I can't say I know what you're going through, but I can imagine how bad that would suck, to know that you may not be here to enjoy even the shitty things life has to offer because at least you'd be here, at least you'd be—"

"Alive," I finished. "I'd be alive."

"So live now," Gabe challenged. "Go kiss that freshman you convinced me you had no feelings for."

"I plan on it." My grin was so wide it hurt.

"Good talk." Gabe laughed. "I'll just show myself out."

"Gabe?" I asked once he reached the door.

He turned and waited.

"Thanks for listening."

He gave me a salute. "Yeah, well, I'm still going to kick your ass if you break her heart."

"Don't worry. I imagine she's going to be the one doing the breaking."

"How do you figure?" He crossed his arms and leaned against the door frame.

"Because in the end, I won't have anything to give her that's worth having."

"Do yourself a favor." Gabe pushed away from the door, "Let her be the one to make that choice in the end. Not you."

I nodded. Yeah, I could do that. I owed her that much, and I'd sure as hell die trying. I smirked at the double meaning.

Gabe waved goodbye and walked off. Who would have thought Gabe had a heart? Or that he was that deep? Just goes to show what you miss in life when you aren't really looking.

Seek, and you'll find.

Act like an ass, and you'll only see your reflection in the mirror.

TWENTY-SIX

Holy crap. I was going to eat turkey in front of Randy Michels. Uncle Jobob was going to flip!

Kiersten

"**H**e got down on bended knee?" Lisa screeched as she ran around my room in a frenzy. "What did you do?"

"I said yes, of course." I laughed, throwing some more clothes into my suitcase. I wasn't really sure what I wanted to bring or wear. Uncle Jo about crapped himself when I told him the plan. He was so happy I was actually doing something that he started crying on the other end of the phone. When I pointed it out, he said a mosquito had flown into his eye. Right, in November.

It also helped matters that he'd idolized Randy Michels for years. I was under strict instructions by my uncle to marry Wes at all costs. He even offered to drive us to Vegas. Yeah, so basically, I had the coolest uncle in the world. Nobody could argue that. He and my aunt were planning a huge celebration with the rest of the family. They were going to Skype me on Turkey Day, so I could say hi to everyone.

"I would have freaked out." Lisa fell onto my bed with a loud sigh. "I mean, I'm freaking out now, and it didn't even happen to me!"

"Right." I tugged a shirt out from underneath her and folded it into my suitcase.

"You're dating Weston Michels." She gave another giggle and then jolted up from her bed, "Oh my gosh! Have you sl—"

"Don't go there." I pointed at her face. "We've kissed, like once — or twice now, actually."

"What?" I swear her scream just woke hibernating bears in Alaska. "And you didn't tell me?"

"I knew," Gabe said from the door, giving me a wink and slapping me on the shoulder as he walked by.

"Helpful, Gabe, thank you." I glared.

Lisa crossed her arms and pouted. "Everyone knew but me?"

"No, Gabe just saw me doing the walk of shame one morning and jumped to conclusions. I had to clear the air; otherwise, he would have assumed the worst, because well, it's Gabe."

"True."

"And the rest is history."

Lisa seemed satisfied with that answer because about two minutes later, she grinned. "Is he a good kisser?"

"Do we have to discuss this now?" Gabe complained. "Wait until I'm not in the room."

"So leave." Lisa shrugged.

"Can't." He pushed her to the side of the bed so he could sit down. "I have to send off my favorite girl. You know, give her all the normal warnings about what guys think, and why she should never under any circumstances watch a movie with a member of the opposite sex after eleven p.m."

"Huh?" I stopped folding clothes. "Why not?"

"Sex." Gabe glared, "Studies show that testosterone skyrockets while watching horror movies, add that into nighttime and touching, and you, my friend, have a recipe for a baby rattle and no future."

Lisa gaped. "Wow, where were you during my sex ed classes in high school?"

"Players know the game well, don't they?" I teased.

"Only the stars." He blew me a kiss and held up his hand for a high five.

Lisa slapped it.

I rolled my eyes at her.

"What?" She shrugged. "He really is so talented in the field."

"And you know this how? Cousins? Remember?"

"Family equals no secrets." Lisa nodded. "And it helps that three sororities rank guys on a scale of one to ten. Care to take a guess about Gabe's rating?"

"Five?" I lifted my eyebrows.

Gabe shot me a glare.

"Eleven." Lisa sounded proud. "They put him in his own ranking."

"I'll probably be president one day." Gabe gave us both cocky grins and patted himself on the back.

"I don't know why, but I feel the need to congratulate you on being a whore. Why does that feel wrong?" I tapped my finger against my chin. "Oh right, because it is. One of these days it's going to catch up with you."

"Never." Gabe shook his head. "A player plays by the rules, knows the game plan, knows every possible strategy and execution. Me getting caught would be like Chuck Norris dying in a stunt. Um, it won't happen. Want to know why? Because he's badass."

"Did you just compare your sexual prowess to Chuck Norris's karate skills?" I asked.

"Same thing." Gabe shrugged.

Shaking my head, I glanced at the clock on my nightstand. "Crap! He's going to be here! Hurry, hurry! I have to put everything in my bag."

"Everything?" Gabe glanced around the room. "Are you planning on moving in?"

Lisa's answer was to smack him on the back of the head. With a growl, he jumped to his feet and started piling stuff in my suitcases. I even caught him try to throw my alarm clock in. Seriously?

"Done!" Lisa sat on the suitcase while Gabe zipped.

"I love you guys," I gushed, pulling them both in for hugs.

Gabe patted my head like I was twelve, and Lisa looked like she was going to cry. You'd think I'd never visited a boy's house before. Oh, wait. Right.

Someone knocked on our door.

Lisa ran out of my room, banging her arm against the sofa as she made her way across the living room, and finally opened up the door.

"Hey, Lisa." Wes grinned and handed her a paper turkey. "Made it myself." He peered around her. "My girlfriend ready?"

And my roommate officially swooned against the door, putting the back of her hand against her forehead. Gabe was going to have to give her CPR.

"Be still, my beating heart!" Lisa said in a southern drawl. "Sugar, your man is here, and he is fine, fine, fine."

"Sorry." Gabe grabbed Lisa by the shoulders and steered her away from Wes. "She forgot to take her meds today."

"It's okay." Wes chuckled and then lifted his eyes. I stared straight back.

Time stilled.

Okay, so maybe it didn't stop, but for some reason, my heart started racing as he took purposeful steps toward me.

First, his hands braced my hips.

And then his mouth found mine.

And it was my turn to swoon.

Gabe and Lisa both whistled, but I didn't care. I wrapped my arms around Wes's neck, pulling him toward me. Mine. He was mine for two weeks, whatever that meant. Boyfriend.

"My man ready?"

He grinned, kissing my nose. "My freshman ready?"

"Low blow." I glared.

"Had to be said." He sighed and kissed my forehead. "I'll grab your suitcase."

Lisa sighed while Gabe smacked her on the arm, just as Wes came into the living room with my giant suitcase.

"You do know I didn't ask you to move in with me, right?" he joked.

"A girl has to be prepared!" Lisa defended me. "And who knows what the Seattle weather will do!"

Wes held up a hand as if to surrender and then nodded toward the door. "Let's go. My crazy dad awaits."

"Onward." I thrust my fist into the air and said goodbye to Gabe and Lisa. I was going to meet the richest man in the world. Awesome, what could go wrong?

TWENTY-SEVEN

Holy shit. I was taking a girl home. Somebody start a fire in Hell — because it's officially frozen over.

Weston

"Y ou nervous?" I asked as we pulled onto Fauntleroy Way in downtown Seattle. It boasted of only twelve houses in the little gated community, meaning we had mega privacy. I swear my dad had cameras everywhere, even at the end of the street, just in case someone sketchy wanted to get a view of one of us in the pool. Not that they could, there was enough landscaping to make the house its own private resort, not to mention the fact that we had over a half-mile of private beach. You know, if you could call a rocky coast a beach. But every summer, we had sand brought in from the tropics. Just to make it look legit.

"A little." Kiersten sighed and looked out the window. "So, which house is yours?"

"Everything you see on this side of the street toward the water? It's all ours."

"Huh?"

"A main house, two cottages, a few tennis courts, a man-made pond, and then that house over there…" I pointed to the far end of the property as the gate opened, making it easier for her to see. "…is where my Oma stays when she visits."

"Uh, Oma?"

"Grandma," I corrected myself. "Sorry, my mom was one hundred percent Dutch, so when I was little, my grandma was Oma."

Kiersten grinned and then sucked in a sharp breath as the second gate opened to the main house. I drove through and tried to imagine what it would look like through her eyes.

At least six thousand square feet, not the largest mansion in the world, all glass windows with sharp angles, allowing for the sun to shine through. It was white and had been remodeled from its original brick form in 1927 to look like an architect's paradise. There were exactly seventeen steps leading to the massive fifteen-foot tall oak entry, and just as I pulled the car to a stop, the butler walked out and opened Kiersten's door.

"Ma'am, we've been expecting you."

"Ronald." I nodded my head in his direction.

He grinned at me. At eighty-two, he was a force to be reckoned with. He wasn't really our butler anymore, since technically he'd retired twenty years ago, but my dad hadn't the heart to let him go, so now he greeted guests, brewed beer in the cottage my dad let him live in rent-free, and basically kept the house running since my mother's death.

"Mr. Weston." Ronald clapped his hands on my shoulder and pulled me in for a hug. "It's been too long; how are you?"

He knew I was sick.

But he never treated me any differently. He just refused to

discuss it — I understood though — everyone in his life was gone. He and my brother had been very close. He'd taken Tye's death really hard, and I knew mine would be just something else that might cause his heart to finally give out.

"Good, I feel great," I lied and hugged him back. "Dad home?"

"In the study waiting." Ronald smiled and clapped twice. Two staff members ran down the stairs to grab our stuff.

I held out my hand to Kiersten. "Ready to meet my dad?"

"Holy crap." She wiped her hands on her jeans before latching on to me. "I feel like I'm about to meet the president or something."

I threw my head back and laughed. "Trust me, it's 'or something.' He's not that intimidating. Promise." I could tell she didn't believe me. Her eyes kept getting wider and wider as we walked farther into the house. The foyer had a bridge-like walkway that went directly toward the main room. A huge bay window let in tons of light from the front; we took a right and went to the study.

"Dad?" I called.

"In here."

I kissed Kiersten's temple as I clenched her hand and led her into the large study. It was decorated in an Old World style, complete with mahogany-wooded walls and matching bookcases.

Dad was sitting behind his large desk, sipping brandy.

"A little early to hit the bottle, eh dad?" I joked.

His eyes narrowed, and then he laughed. "Yes, well, I just fired Alfred, so I imagine I'm allowed to drink."

"What?" Alfred had been one of my dad's closest advisors for years. "What for?"

"Embezzlement."

I cleared my throat and nodded toward Kiersten.

Dad waved me off. "Surely it's hit CNN by now." He tapped his desk as a flat-screen descended from the West Wall. Sure enough, as soon as the TV came on, there was news about the scandal.

"So." Dad turned off the TV. "Who is this lovely creature?"

"Kiersten." She held out her hand. "It's nice to meet you, sir."

"Sir?" My dad's brows furrowed. "Do I look eighty?"

"Er, no?" She gave him a shaky smile.

"Randy." His eyes twinkled. "You can call me Randy, just don't call me Dad. It may cause a heart attack. I can't imagine this one settling down yet." He pointed at me and shuddered. "Poor boy can barely do his laundry and tie his shoes."

"Hilarious." I rolled my eyes.

"You can cook, can't you?" Randy crossed his arms. "I mean, that's why you brought her, right, son? To cook Thanksgiving dinner?"

I knew he was kidding.

Kiersten, however, didn't.

Wide-eyed and pale, she stared at him as her mouth dropped open and then closed again. She looked at me with a hint of panic in her eyes.

I kept a straight face, as did Dad.

"I, um…" Kiersten released my hand and tucked her hair behind her ear, a move I'd come to recognize as a nervous tick. She was freaking out. "I could totally put something together. I can't promise it'll taste like what you're used to, but I can try."

Damn, she was a sweetheart.

"Where'd you say you got her?" Dad said, completely

ignoring her answer.

"College."

"She's smart."

"I know." I put my arm around her.

"And sweet," Dad pointed out, walking around his desk. "And dare I say… beautiful."

"All things I'm very aware of. It's why I stole her away."

"Smart man." Dad chuckled and winked at Kiersten. "Dear girl, you don't have to cook; I was joking. It's all I have for entertainment these days with Wes gone all the time and his bro—"

Dad's face went pale. "His brother is no longer with us, as I'm sure you already knew. So I do get lonely. I apologize if I made you uncomfortable."

"No problem." She smiled warmly and patted his forearm. His eyebrow lifted as he offered his arm.

She took it, beaming up at him as if he was the damn sun.

"Now…" Dad cleared his throat, making a nice recovery. "Why don't we get you settled in your room, and we'll let Wes get us something cold to drink. You do know you're welcome to stay the entire break. We love visitors, and anything you need, I'll be sure to have Melda—" He stopped talking to Kiersten and yelled, "Melda!"

"Here, sir." Melda came around the corner, demure as ever. She was Ronald's wife, also late in her years, but the best cook in the known universe.

"Melda here…" Dad gestured and then directed his attention back to Kiersten, "…will be sure to get you anything you desire. Hot chocolate? Coffee?"

"Coffee." Kiersten nodded. "Never hot chocolate."

"Son," Dad called back to me. "Find me one about twenty-five years older, and we'll talk."

Kiersten frowned in confusion. "One?"

"A beautiful lady, such as yourself." Dad released her hand, kissed it again, and nodded in my direction. "I think I'll stop hogging you and allow my son to give you the grand tour. I'll get the drinks."

"Thank you." Kiersten grinned warmly.

Dad smiled warmly in our direction and walked off.

"I love him," Kiersten said once he was out of earshot.

"So does the rest of the world." I chuckled.

"No…" Kiersten put her hand on my arm. "He's amazing. You're so lucky to have him. Really. I would do anything to… well, you already know that. You're just lucky."

Not really. I mean, yes, I was damned lucky to have an awesome dad. I was even more lucky that my dad was loaded enough to get me the best drugs but lucky? I didn't feel lucky. Not when I was giving Kiersten her first and last tour of my house. I knew how girls worked; the little wheels in her head would be turning 'round and 'round, imagining Christmases, birthdays, all normal celebrations. Hell, even New Year's.

I hadn't told anyone yet, but when I thought about 2014… When I thought about New Year's, I couldn't actually picture myself here. It was as if I was a shadow, no longer existing, but watching from a distance.

The sad part was the minute I watched Kiersten and my dad, I could see her years from now, still charming parents, possibly meeting her future in-laws, and it killed me inside. It actually made me think I was having another bout of nausea from my drugs, but it was all self-inflicted because, again, I was reminded of what I would be missing. And it wasn't the silly things like playing football or getting a bowl game this year.

It was her.

And that made me want to fight even more. Just like Gabe said. I could do this. I could beat it. I'd sure as hell try. In the past, fighting for football or for school had never been a huge pull for me.

But beating this for her?

Yeah. I'd fight demons for her. I'd fight the darkness in me, the sickness. I'd fight that damn tumor. And I'd live. Because I sure as hell wanted a 2014 with that girl in my arms.

TWENTY-EIGHT

Words aren't really coming at this point. I mean, I knew he was basically a billionaire but...everything seems so normal, so wonderful. I feel like I'm waiting for the ball to drop. Why do I keep feeling that way?

Kiersten

Overwhelmed didn't even begin to describe how I felt. I had my own bathroom, with a rain shower, heated tile, a heated towel rack, a flat-screen TV. I mean, seriously, I could go on and on. I even Facetimed Uncle Jo so he could see everything.

He gasped like I knew he would. Pretty soon, I had Uncle Jo, my aunt, and their two dogs, all gaping at the iPhone screen as I slowly did a panoramic shot of the bathroom. Wow, how lame, I was actually taking pictures of someone else's bathroom like a complete and total stalker.

"Can I move there?" Uncle Jo asked. Aunt San swatted him across the chest while he chuckled and asked again. The dogs barked. I missed them. Before I knew it, I started to get emotional. What had I been thinking these past two years?

Locking myself in my room to grieve when I had a family waiting outside the whole time.

"You okay?" Uncle Jo asked when I took him off Facetime and pressed the phone to my ear.

"Yeah." I sighed. "Just really thankful for you guys. I love you."

"We love you too, kiddo. Now, get off the phone and take lots of pictures so I can live through you, okay?"

"Deal." I laughed and said goodbye, hanging up the phone and walking around my giant bedroom. It had a deck that overlooked the Puget Sound. It was also bigger than five of my rooms back home. It had a large over-stuffed bed, and I'm pretty sure if I snapped my fingers, an iPod would turn on.

A knock sounded on the door, and then it opened.

"Good thing I wasn't changing." I joked as Wes stepped in.

"Damn." He grinned. "I was hoping I'd catch you unaware."

"Clever."

He stalked toward me. "I thought so."

I turned my attention back to the water. The view was so pretty, and for it being Thanksgiving, it wasn't all too cold outside.

Wes went and took a seat in one of the deck chairs and then patted his knee. I shook my head no.

He smiled. Seriously that's all it took. One smile, and I was putty, absolutely useless against his magic boy powers. With a heavy sigh — you know, to show my disapproval at his manipulation — I sat on his lap and leaned back against his chest.

"Thank you," he whispered into my hair after a few silent minutes, "for coming with me."

"Pretty sure it should be me thanking you." I linked my

hands in his. "And thanks for being my boyfriend for two weeks."

He tensed.

"What? You did say two weeks, right?" I elbowed him in the ribs. "I mean, you're throwing me a bone. That's it, right?"

"No." He turned me in his lap. "No bone, no pity dates. I want you…" His hand caressed my face gently, his fingertips grazing my skin and then pulling back as if the contact was too much for him to handle. "I like you a lot."

"So… the two weeks is up for discussion?" I joked.

He swallowed, staring into my eyes as if searching for something, "I'll tell you what…" His voice cracked. "I'll give you as much time as I have."

"As much time as you have." I searched his face trying to figure out why he would say it like that. "Are you planning on not having much time?"

He looked straight through me. It was as if he had seen a ghost, his face went pale, and his eyes watered.

"Sure," I answered quickly. "As much time as you have."

"Promise?" He jerked his head away and looked out at the ocean. "Promise me?"

"I promise."

"Good." His smile returned, he kissed me on the cheek. "Let's go get dinner then. I'm sure dad's hungry, and you've had a long day. We can watch a movie later, all right?"

"Sounds good." I hopped off his lap but didn't release his hand; for some reason, it seemed important. Important that I touch him as much as possible. How crazy did that sound? I felt this urgency to be near him as if he was going to disappear at any minute. Wow, who was insecure now? I pushed the thought out of my head and swore to myself I wasn't going to overthink it. I liked him, he liked me, and I officially had more than two weeks. I knew it was like we were moving fast, but I really liked him, and I knew in my heart two weeks would never be enough. Actually, I was pretty sure that whole year wouldn't be enough. Summer might just ruin me if I didn't get to see him at least once. Who knew? Maybe I could take summer school so I could be close by; that was if he wasn't bored with me by then.

Dinner went by smoothly. You know, if smooth meant I couldn't decide which fork to use with my salad and which one to use with the salmon. At one point, Mr. Michels, or Randy as he preferred I call him, began showing me which utensil to use by lifting it high in the air and diving into his food. I kind of loved him. He had Wes's fun personality but still seemed to be grounded.

I was stuffed by the time the meal was done.

"And now…" Randy pushed back his chair. "I bid you farewell. Tomorrow we have turkey, and I'm watching football."

"Amen," Wes said.

"Um, Wes, can I talk to you for a minute?"

"Sure." Wes pushed away from the table and followed his dad into the hall.

I couldn't hear what they were saying, but at one point, it looked like Randy was trying to feel Wes's pulse. Weird. They seemed to be arguing, and then Randy swore and pinched the bridge of his nose and walked off. Wes's shoulders slumped as he slammed his fist against the wall, not hard, but hard enough to show that he was upset.

"Everything okay?" I asked in a small voice, coming up behind him.

His eyes scanned the house as if memorizing it one last time. "Yeah, just father-son stuff. Football stuff, really." Wes shrugged. "No biggie. Hey—" He flashed me another killer smile. "Let's go watch a movie."

"Cool."

When he said movie, I thought he meant in the living room.

Not a theater room.

With popcorn and reclining seats.

From here on out, when I think of Heaven, this is the picture I'm going to have in my head. Sitting with Wes in our own private movie theater, at his house, holding his hand.

"Any movie, but it has to be a Christmas movie." He clicked through the Apple TV. "You pick."

"Why Christmas?"

"I love Christmas." He shrugged. "And I may not be around for Christmas this year, at least not in this house, so I thought it'd be nice to watch."

"Where are you going to be?"

"Oh, we have other houses around the area, just depends on my dad's mood which one we stay at."

"How awful for you," I teased.

"My cross, my burden. Now pick." He flipped me the remote and put his hands behind his head.

"I choose…" I clicked through. "This one."

He squinted at the screen. "You're kidding."

"You said any Christmas movie, and I believe you said lady's choice."

"It's Mickey Mouse."

"My favorite Christmas movie. You gonna go back on your word?"

"You really are my little lamb, aren't you? All innocent, wanting to watch Mickey Mouse Christmas." He reached out and stroked my face. "Tell me it's wrong to want to blot out all that purity… right here, right now."

"It's wrong," I said simply, ignoring the buzzing in my head as his fingers ran down the side of my cheek.

He sighed and pulled back. "Fine, the lamb speaks, Big Bad Wolf listens."

"As it should be." I leaned into him and then moved the armrest so I could truly lay across him.

"And then Lamb tempts Wolf," Wes said in a low voice.

"And Wolf rises above temptation," I sang.

"Wolf likes temptation."

"Wolf needs to watch the movie."

"Lamb needs to stop talking before Wolf silences her with his teeth."

My grin was so huge, I swear I couldn't see out of my own eyes as I laughed and turned away from him. "Stop!"

"Not used to hearing that particular word. Whatever does it mean?"

"It means no." I pushed at his hand as it rested on my hip and lifted my shirt to touch bare skin.

"Hmm, what's no mean?"

"It means…" The movie suddenly blasted across the screen.

Wes leaned down and spoke against my ear, "Saved by the Mouse."

TWENTY-NINE

I should have walked away. Instead, I blocked the way, made myself so impossible to walk away from that it was too late. Late, early, not that it mattered, time wasn't on my side, and she wouldn't be either, not when I told her.

Weston

She fell asleep in my arms during the first fifteen minutes. I closed my eyes, not because I was tired, but because it felt normal. I could almost imagine it was normal. I'd taken my girlfriend home for the holidays, we got bored, watched a movie, and she fell asleep.

But it wasn't.

I checked my watch.

I needed to take more meds, so as much as it killed me to move that gorgeous girl away from me — it was time for bed. I picked up a piece of hair and examined it, twisting it between my fingers. It wasn't an obsession with hair; it was more of an obsession with everything that made her unique. Her red hair, her smile, her laugh, the way she pushed people away — the way she let me in.

Damn. I was screwed, so damn screwed.

She would find out soon. I'd have to tell her. I had one game left, and then Coach was going to bench me. He said I wasn't the same player I used to be. I couldn't argue that. Not with me puking at practice every day. I knew I was letting the team down, but it was better to step down from the entire team than to allow them to get their asses kicked or, worse, allow any of them to get hurt because I couldn't hold my shit together anymore.

I just hadn't realized Coach would call my dad or that my dad would tell him I was sick.

"Sick?" Coach had asked, "Well, will he get better?"

My dad hadn't said anything because he didn't know, just like I didn't know, just like the doctors didn't know.

He'd argued with me about it again. Wanting me to at least see if the tumor was shrinking. I didn't want to know. Who the hell would? I had a freaking tumor twisting its way dangerously close to my heart, and they wanted to know if it was growing?

Hell. No.

I'd rather live in ignorance than see the scan of that monster inside my chest. If the drugs weren't shrinking it, chances were, I'd die in surgery or come out of it and be made comfortable.

Dad didn't know, but I was going to ask the doctors about that.

Why would I want to live through surgery? Only to die a few months later in pain?

Maybe that made me a coward. Hell, I felt like one most days. Especially as the days got closer to my surgery. I had three more weeks until D-day. Three more weeks to either tell Kiersten the truth or break her damn heart.

What the hell had I been thinking to give her as much

time as I had left? Her eyes had lit up. I knew she was thinking that was a great promise. It was all I freaking had to give her.

Time was the most precious thing in the world to me, and I'd just given her all of it. Because I was falling for her. Because I cared for her. Because I wanted to give her something to remember me by, even if it would eventually fade like its namesake. Time... what an absolute horror-inducing word.

THIRTY

I wish I could forget the dreams... I wish I could be with him every night. And here I thought the nightmares were gone.

Kiersten

I woke up screaming. And then, for reasons I really didn't want to dig into, let alone discuss with that logical part of my brain that normally made good decisions, I padded my way to Wes's room.

Just as I lifted my hand to knock, the door swung open.

And I stared slack-jawed at that amazing eight-pack. Was I sighing? Yes. Biting my cheek to keep from grinning like a fool? Absolutely. I took my time looking, and my nightmare was officially forgotten.

"Feeling better?" Wes tilted my chin up so that he could see my face.

"How did you know I was feeling bad?" I asked in a sleepy voice.

He sighed and opened the door for me so I could walk in. "I heard you screaming."

"Oh."

I looked down at his clenched fists and felt instantly guilty. Embarrassment washed over me as I took a step back. His hands came around my waist, lifting me into the air. In an instant, I was lying on his bed.

"No, it's fine. I'm sorry. I didn't mean to wake you. The nightmare's gone and—" I struggled to get up from the bed, but he held me firm in his arms.

Wes brushed a kiss against my forehead. "You didn't let me finish." He gave me a sexy grin. "I was on my way to your room to beat whatever monsters were hiding under your bed."

"You slay dragons now?"

"Is that what you dream about?" He pulled me against him, so we were lying chest to chest. "Dragons?"

"I wish." I shuddered in his arms. "A lot of times, I dream about death, about my parents' death. They're drowning, and I can't reach them. I'm always too late."

Wes's grip tightened around my waist, his breathing seemed to pick up. Licking his lips, he kissed my forehead. "Time's a bitch, isn't it?"

I laughed. "Yeah, it really is."

"If only I would have done this, I should have done this, I could have done this..." He swore. "Life is full of those three."

"Three?"

"Woulda, shoulda, coulda." Wes traced my jaw with his fingertip. "It's human nature to assume that we have that sort of control over what happens to us, but the truth is... life happens, and sometimes you're too late. Hell, sometimes you're too early. Sometimes you make the wrong choice just like sometimes you make the right one. The only time people ever use those three is when things don't go the right way.

People don't question themselves when things are going well. They question themselves when things have gone to hell."

I hadn't really thought about that.

"You can spend your life in that zone, thinking you have even a sliver of control over things that you have no power over. Rather than concentrating on what you should have done, concentrate on what you can do now."

"And what's that?" I asked breathlessly.

"Kiss your totally sexy and wise boyfriend…" He kissed my nose. "Let him slay your dragons." His lips moved to my cheek. "And know that in this moment… you're not living in the woulda, shoulda, coulda zone. You're exactly where the universe wants you to be."

"In your bed?" I grinned.

"Nah." His mouth met mine. "In my arms."

Breath hissed out of my mouth as he pressed his lips against mine. Everything about him was so warm and alive. I pressed my hands against his chest, loving the way his skin felt against my fingertips.

He pulled back, eyes closed, and swore, clenching my hands to his chest as if they were his lifeline as if my touch was somehow changing his world.

"I can feel you," he whispered. "I love having your hands here." His eyes opened, but it didn't look like Wes. It looked like a ghost of him, as if he wasn't really present with me but somewhere far away. "I wish I could be whole for you."

"Whole?" I slid my hands to his shoulders and pulled him closer. "You gonna tell me you're half a man?"

He hesitated and then shrugged. "Nah, just wish I could be totally yours, only yours. I wish I could get a do-over."

"A do-over?" I pulled away and lay. "Weren't you just

spouting nonsense about woulda, coulda, shoulda?"

"Right." He laughed. "Thanks, smartass." A pillow landed on my face before I could stop it. I pushed it away and sat up as he did the same.

"All I'm saying…" He sighed as if he had the world on his shoulders. "…is that I wish all my firsts and lasts were with you and only you."

"Bummer." I sighed. "I wasn't the first freshman you kissed?"

"Actually…" He smiled thoughtfully. "You were."

"Mission accomplished. And I better be the last freshman you kiss." I jammed my finger in his chest as he winced and threw the pillow again.

"First, last, only." He bit down on his lower lip. "Favorite."

"Oh wow, you must want me to have good dreams tonight then; you're really laying it on thick."

"Just covering my bases."

"Oh yeah?"

"What?" He pointed down at himself. "I'm not dream material?"

"Point Wes." I held up one finger.

Grinning, he reared back and pounced on me, pressing my back against the pillows and the bed as he hovered over me.

"What if my dream turns into a nightmare?"

His face fell. "What do you mean?"

"What if you're in the dream and I can't reach you?"

"Close your eyes."

"What?"

"Just do it."

"Fine." Humoring him, I closed my eyes and waited. His lips tickled my ear as he began to whisper.

"Every time you close your eyes, regardless of where I am or where you are, I want you to remember this." His fingers laced with mine, and then he pressed my hand against my own chest. "Wherever I am, whatever I'm doing, alive or dead, young or old, my heart will always be with yours. Every beat you feel against your fingertips…" His finger tapped against my chest, once, twice. "…is me calling out to you. It's you returning the call. It's us talking, communicating, bonding, sharing. Living — Kiersten, it's us living. There may come a time in your life when your heart will have to beat for mine… but you'll have to carry on if I can't. Just like there may come a time when I have to do the same for you. But in the end, one of us will always carry on this." He tapped again. "So there's never a reason to be afraid of running out of time — because we keep our own."

I couldn't trust myself to speak, not after what he'd just said. Wes had single-handedly put me at ease, as well as wisely taught me one thing. Control what you can, love what you can, and the rest, well… the rest was just the rest. So I couldn't reach my parents? I tapped my fingertips against his chest. Well, I could feel Wes, and he was right. We were keeping our own time, making our own — living.

"Sleep," Wes murmured. "I've exhausted you with my gibberish."

"Not true!" I yawned.

Wes laughed and kissed my mouth. "Very true. Now, I want you to close your eyes while I hold you and keep watch."

"Watch?"

"For the damn dragons!" he teased. "Don't worry, I won't let them take your virtue."

"Right." I laughed. "Because dragons are known to do that."

"Never trust a lizard."

"Uh, methinks dragons aren't technically lizards."

"Sure they are." He turned my body so that he was spooning me. "Just like dinosaurs. Trust me on this, I'm a senior."

"Sure you aren't a super senior?" I yawned again.

"Go to sleep." He nibbled on my ear a bit and then sighed, causing goosebumps to jump to life around my body.

Right, like I could sleep with him touching me like that. My eyes felt heavy as he continued to rain kisses down my neck, and then I allowed my body to fall into that heavy wave of sleep — in Wes's arms.

THIRTY-ONE

So apparently, I'm boring... Awesome.

Weston

I wasn't sure what was more disconcerting, the fact that in the span of a few hours, Kiersten had fallen asleep twice on me or the fact that I'd been kissing her the last time she'd done it.

Clearly, she hadn't been sleeping well.

She'd asked me about keeping time — our time. Apparently, she liked that. I couldn't lie to myself — I loved that idea. It made everything seem more permanent when it was anything but that.

I shifted away from her and looked up at my ceiling. The same ceiling I'd been staring at all my life.

A soft sigh escaped Kiersten's mouth as she twisted in her sleep and then threw her arm over my chest, stealing the breath from my body. Damn, but that girl could pack a punch if she wanted.

"Wes…" she mumbled, her head twisting from side to side. In an instant, I was pulling her close to me again. I wasn't sure if it was guilt eating me alive or my sickness; really, it was a toss-up at that point. I was making her fall harder, and it wasn't like I was being anything but myself. I wasn't lying; I wasn't trying to get her to sleep with me, at least not in a sexual way — it was the first time in my life I was actually being real.

Great timing, I know.

"Wes." Her lips found my bare shoulder. She may as well have just stabbed me; I felt that kiss, those lips, her wet tongue all the way up and down my body like a shot of heroin to my system. I'd never done drugs, but I could imagine that this was what it felt like.

Kiersten's leg lifted and then went between mine.

Shit.

No way out of that one. I was going to have to suffer an entire night with the girl plastered against me and gain no relief in the process. Okay, so maybe I knew exactly what a heroin addict felt like. Hell, I wanted to take a hit, I wanted to drink her in, but I knew, if I made that choice for her — she'd end up hating me. I don't care what girls say; no innocent chick goes into a relationship thinking it's just a one-time thing unless they're sluts. They expect forever.

The one thing I knew I couldn't give.

"Sleep." I kissed her forehead again and held onto her as tight as I could.

"Wake up, sunshine, time for turkey," I whispered into Kiersten's hair. She looked like a really hot version of Cousin It. Her red hair was wrapped all around my pillow, my arm, my face, her face; it was like its own person with its own zip code and inability to stay in its personal space. And I loved the hell out of it. I parted the red locks and found an eye.

"There you are."

The eye narrowed.

"So, still not a morning person?" I asked.

Didn't think it was possible, but the eye narrowed more until I was convinced it was closed. I pulled the curtain of hair farther back. Two eyes. Score! She wasn't blind.

"Why are you staring at me as if you just discovered gravity?"

"I did." I smirked.

"This better be good."

"You."

"Huh?"

I sighed. "Still too early for my innuendos and all around amazing pickup lines, huh?" I swatted her with the pillow. "Get up, Lamb; Wolf's hungry, and I've had to pee for like five hours."

"So why didn't you go?"

"Because a ninja masquerading as my girlfriend was holding me hostage against my own bed all night." I nodded to her legs as they intertwined with mine. "Not to mention the fact that her viselike grip was so damn cute I just stayed put."

"Wes." She jolted up. "I'm sorry! I'm normally not a—"

"Clinger?" I offered.

There went that eye narrowing again. I wondered if I was

losing points by actually being a morning person. I hadn't taken any drugs yet, mainly because I physically couldn't move, so I wanted to soak up the happiness while I still wanted to talk to a person rather than my porcelain toilet.

"Don't you dare start calling me clinger." She moaned and covered her face with her hands. "Sorry for pinning you to the bed all night."

I smirked and licked my lips. "Yeah, there are worse ways to go."

Like the doctor using you as his own version of Operation. Only when he touches the edges you bleed out, and your heart stops, no do-overs, no second tries.

"You okay?" Kiersten touched my shoulder. I hadn't realized I'd zoned out. Clearly, the fact that I just got handed my football jersey and was another few weeks closer to surgery was messing with me, not to mention the fact that I kind of wanted to live.

Every reason keeping my feet firmly planted on earth was living and breathing next to me, damn it.

"Stellar," I sang. "But I still have to use the bathroom, so if you could just untangle your long sexy legs from mine, I'd appreciate it. Actually, I'd appreciate it more if you just let me have my way with—"

An exasperated sigh exploded from Kiersten's lips.

"The toilet," I finished. "That's all I ask."

"Fine." She laughed and moved fully away from me, probably the most alone and lost I'd felt in years. Irritating to think that one person had that much power over my attitude.

"Why don't you go get ready in the other bathroom, and we'll meet downstairs in a bit for some awesome breakfast?"

"Okay." Kiersten slowly shuffled across the large rug that

covered the hardwood floors in my room. "Wes?" She turned.

I stopped, my hand on the doorknob to my connecting bathroom. "Yeah?"

"Thank you." A bright blush stained her cheeks. "For last night. For chasing the monsters away…"

"Anytime. It's kind of my job to protect you."

"A job sounds like you're forced."

"Nah," I argued. "Saying it's my job just means it's my identity in a way. You know how people go, 'Hey, I'm Rick. I'm a janitor.'" I smiled. "Now I can say, hey, I'm Weston, and I kill monsters on behalf of my very sexy girlfriend so she can sleep at night."

"Lame." Her laugh hit me in all the right and wrong places, making the idea of using the restroom a moot point. I wanted to stay pinned, preferably beneath her.

"Nah, heroic," I argued. "Now, go get ready so we can eat cinnamon rolls."

Apparently, that's all I needed to say. Her eyes widened, and then she was running down the hall. Good to know she was a fan of breakfast. That could have been a deal-breaker right there. I hated it when chicks refused to eat the most important meal of the day. As if they didn't realize how much it helped. I knew, mainly because my pills ripped my insides to shreds if I didn't eat.

I closed and locked the door behind me and opened the cupboard under the sink. Fifteen bottles, all with my name on them. Hell, I almost wished I was a druggy. You know, one of those guys who stole oxy and morphine to get high.

Right. I never even touched my pain pills. They numbed my senses so much that it wasn't worth it, and it wasn't like I was in any pain. My doc said it would help me with the anxiety.

Clearly, he'd never heard of exercise. All oxy did was turn me into one of those zombies from Walking Dead, only I was pretty sure I looked more haggard and scary.

I popped the lid off of my first pill bottle, dropped the pill into my hand, and shook my head. It was a powerful little bitch. I actually nicknamed it *bitch* because it was so small that you'd think it wouldn't do much damage. Wrong. The first time I took it, I was sick for a week straight. I became so dehydrated from puking, I had to go to the hospital. Now I know how to take it. I had to take it with my anti-nausea pill, which worked only sixty percent of the time, and then pop my giant ass white pill — the special chemo pill that's made specifically for me.

I had five more pills to take, but I needed to eat first. I quickly jumped in the shower, brushed my teeth, and was dressed, all within fifteen minutes.

I checked my watch. Kiersten was probably just getting ready. I didn't want her to see me taking any pills — I didn't feel right lying to her face when she asked me why I was taking an entire medicine cabinet full of rainbow-colored chemicals, so I stuffed them in my pocket and told myself not to forget to take them after breakfast.

If I did… well, I'd be absolutely no fun for the remainder of break, not to mention it just gave that cranky tumor one more day without a defense, meaning it would grow… and the idea that its tentacles were slowly choking parts of my heart was a mental picture I could really do without.

THIRTY-TWO

I would never get the mental picture out of my head — Wes was hot, his body was ridiculous, and I'd slept plastered against him all night. Oh gosh, I probably even drooled. Well, here's to hoping he still wanted to be my boyfriend after I clung to him like a twelve-year-old Justin Bieber fan. Yay.

Kiersten

I got lost twice on my way down to the kitchen. The first time I went left instead of right, the second time, I was distracted by the middle of the stairway where a few family pictures hung. Wes and his brother stood side by side. They almost looked like twins. My heart clenched a bit when I thought of how awful it would be to lose your brother to something like suicide. You'd probably live to regret every single conversation, every single moment you could have said something different, possibly changed the outcome. I shuddered and went down the wrong side of the staircase leading into the master bedroom.

Crap. Finally, I made my way back up the stairway and down again to the other side, where I could smell the cinnamon wafting from the kitchen. Yeah, I could learn to live with Wes's life. Waking up to fresh rolls in the morning after I sleep in a mansion. Right, life should be so hard; the guy had no idea how lucky he was.

Laughter floated from the kitchen.

Feeling like I was interrupting, I cleared my throat while I walked in. Wes was standing in the corner with Melda, who were frosting rolls and joking with each other.

The kitchen was full of food. Everywhere I looked, the granite counters were covered with different boxes of things, plates, silverware, chips, dips. Crap, were we throwing a Thanksgiving party?

"Kiersten!" Wes crooked his finger. "Come here."

Smiling, I made my way over and stopped right in front of him. He lifted his frosting covered finger to my lips and whispered, "Open."

Well, I wasn't really in a position to say no. My stomach clenched; it was so hungry. I opened my mouth as his finger swiped frosting across my lips, and then my tongue wrapped around the frosting, sucking on his finger until it was gone.

His eyes darkened as he pulled his finger away and then touched his lips to mine. I heard someone clearing a throat, but really all I cared about was the fact that Wes's lips were pressed against mine. He tasted like coffee and sugar, and wow, what I wouldn't give to spend every morning with that taste in my mouth.

"Ahem," Melda said again.

We broke apart. I could feel my face erupt into flames. Wes bit down on his lower lip and looked innocently at Melda. "Sorry, Kiersten's just a messy eater. I was helping her clean up."

"So that's what the kids are calling it these days." Melda's eyebrows rose as she stirred the remaining frosting and dropped it onto the last few rolls. "Now, I only have one rule for Thanksgiving."

"What?" I asked, reaching for a roll.

"Stay out of the kitchen." She smiled, and the wrinkles around her eyes crinkled with mischief. "Young Wes used to hide in the cupboards and scare me. Just last year, Wes tried it again, and I spilled turkey all over the floor." The twinkle left her eyes as she wrung her hands together and licked her lips.

"Tragic death for that bird." Wes shook his head and pulled Melda into his arms. "I promise we'll be good."

"You." Melda poked his chest, clearly forgetting her sadness. "Stay away from this area. I'll call you when I need you, until then, try to occupy yourself."

Wes's eyes turned to mine. "Hmm, I think I can find something to occupy myself."

Pretty sure I was that something. Not that I cared. He held out his hand, I gripped it like a lifeline.

Melda shook her head and handed Wes a large plate full of rolls. "Here you go. Why don't you go into the breakfast room and have some protein and juice. I've set up the breakfast bar for you two, so you won't have any excuses to come back in here."

"She's really thought of everything." I laughed.

"Thanksgiving is her favorite holiday. She doesn't want me ruining it." Wes took my hand and led me into another large room different than the one we ate in last night. "And this is the breakfast room."

The room was entirely covered in windows on the east side. The sun was already up, but I could tell why they ate there in the morning. It was beautiful and warm, almost like a sunroom.

"Juice?" Wes called from behind me.

"Sure." I went over to the table and sat facing the windows.

"So." Wes rubbed his hands together. "You ready to knock some more things off that list of yours?"

I took a sip of juice and nearly cried. It was the perfect mixture of sweet and pulp. "We gonna go bungee jumping on Thanksgiving?"

"Nah." Wes put some of the roll in his mouth. "We're going to skinny dip."

I choked on my juice.

"Of course, we can't do that in broad daylight. After all, what would Melda say? Swimming lessons first, nakedness second."

"I'm almost afraid to ask what third is." I didn't chance looking at him and losing my composure. I mean, I hadn't kissed a guy before him.

"Kiersten," he purred, his lips close to my ear. "You mean to tell me you don't know what comes after being naked?"

Oh. My. Hell. Somebody open a window. His hand grazed my arm as he chuckled deeply into my ear. My body was tense with nervousness and anticipation as his hand made its way up to my shoulder, and then he cupped my neck pulling me closer, so our lips were nearly touching.

"Cranberry sauce."

"Wh-what?" I shook my head. "That comes after being naked?"

Wes's eyes lit up. "Of course, I mean that is how you wrote the list, right? Or am I missing a few in between?" He tapped his fingers against his lips. "Maybe I have it mixed up, but I'm pretty sure you still haven't done that."

I shook my head no, not trusting myself to speak.

"Then it's settled."

"Right." My voice was hoarse. "Swimming. Naked. Cranberry sauce."

"SNC."

"Awesome, like a code."

Wes pulled back and popped some more food into his mouth. "Exactly." He reached into his pocket, and then his gaze furrowed for a few brief seconds before he pulled something out and kept it in his hand.

My eyes were trained on his hand as he kept it clenched tight.

Weird.

I turned my head and looked back out at the Puget Sound.

"So…" Wes's hands were both empty as he braced himself on either side of my chair, his hands massaging my shoulders. "What do you say we eat some more breakfast and then go get ready for a morning swim?"

"Is it going to be cold?" I asked like a five-year-old, not wanting to take swimming lessons.

"Heated pool," Wes answered. "Besides, it's not as if you won't have me to warm you up."

"Probably shouldn't be doing any warming when we're naked."

"You sure about that?" His hands froze on my shoulders. Holy crap, what was I supposed to say?

"I mean, that's wilderness 101, naked bodies rubbing together to create heat, friction—"

"Good thing we aren't in the wilderness." I laughed, trying to kill the sexual tension that was making me want to turn around and throw myself at him.

"I'd say it's a pity." Wes's hands left my shoulders. I almost slumped over onto my plate but kept my body rigid. "Need a suit? I can grab you an extra if you do."

I didn't even want to think about why they would have extra suits.

"Lots of parties, people leave suits. All of them are clean, I promise."

"Yeah." I swallowed. "A suit would be good then."

He was gone for maybe five minutes before he returned with a white bikini. Surely that wasn't all they had left?

My eyes narrowed.

He grinned. "What are you waiting for? Take it."

"Will it cover anything?"

"The important parts." He held it out to me. "Come on, live a little."

I snatched it from his grip. "If I die from hypothermia…"

"Not possible." Wes shrugged. "Not unless you decide to take a midnight swim in the Sound, and I would advise against it since that giant squid seems to think it's a cool place to live."

"Noted." Did I mention I hated fish? Or the fact that the reason I didn't ever go diving with my parents was because water terrified me? Maybe that's why the nightmares were worse for me than someone else. I couldn't imagine dying a watery death. I was terrified of it. Ever since I fell in the pool when I was three, I hadn't been able to go near it without feeling weak in the knees.

Well, Wes would find out soon why this was on my list, so I might as well tell him before I jumped into the water and made a fool out of myself. I went into the bathroom and shakily took off my clothes, then donned the white bikini. Little triangles covered my boobs, just barely, and the bottoms were strings tied to little patches for the front and back. Holy crap, I looked like a prostitute. I mean, the suit looked fine for a stripper.

I leaned against the porcelain sink and took a few deep breaths. I could do this. I would do this. I was halfway through my list.

"Get it together, Kiersten." I stared at my reflection in the mirror; my red hair hung down to the middle of my back in thick waves. My blue eyes stared back in a terrified fashion as if my insides were begging me not to go through with it.

"I can do this," I repeated, my fingers still clutching the sink. "I will do this." With a final jerk, I pulled away from the counter and opened the door. I shook the entire way down the hall. By the time I reached the door to the back porch and pool, my hands were shaking so bad it looked like I was a druggie in need of a hit.

"You can do this," I whispered again and opened the door.

Cold air hit me immediately. Whose brilliant idea was it again to go swimming in November? Oh, right, mine. Teeth chattering, I walked over to the edge of the pool and nearly had a heart attack when Wes's hand touched my shoulder.

"Ready?" he asked.

No. I swallowed and gave him one jerky nod.

With an understanding smile, he pulled me into his warm embrace. His body was searing against mine, the only thing dividing us was our suits, and quite honestly, it scared the heck out of me that I wanted nothing between us, that I wanted to be pressed against him and only him. I could almost forget about the pool, forget about the terror.

"Don't be afraid," he whispered in my hair. "I've got you."

"Promise?"

"I promise, I won't let you fall, not on your own. I won't

let you drown. I won't release your hand until you're ready, and even then, I won't turn my back on you until you're safely back on the ground."

"Okay."

"Really?" He stepped back.

"Yes, just we need to be fast."

"Ah, music to every man's ears." He laughed aloud and helped me step into the pool.

THIRTY-THREE

She has absolutely no idea what she does to me... She's my medicine, my cure, my everything. If only hearts could heal that way — through someone else's beating.

Weston

"**T**here you go." I helped her down the first stair into the giant pool. It was one of those infinity ones; at first glance, it looked like the pool ran directly into the Sound instead of off a nice little cliff leading to the hot tub.

"It's warm." Kiersten splashed her feet a bit and looked up at me, the brightest, sexiest smile I'd ever seen on her lips. It was hopeful and completely trusting in me and in us. I should have told her then. Told her that I wasn't the hero she thought I was. Nah, I was keeping something epic from her, which sort of made me the villain in this tale. But damn, I wanted to be the hero. Gabe's words haunted me.

"*Don't tell her.*" His damn voice blared in my head, reminding me that I needed to let her make her own decisions, that when the ball did drop, I allowed it to stay in her court, not mine.

"Do yourself a favor. Let her be the one to make that choice in the end, not you."

Kiersten wasn't like other girls; she probably wouldn't run away from me. No, she'd cling. She'd make me feel worse about my future, and in the end, she'd hate me for taking away her choice. I didn't—

"Wes?" Kiersten's hand cupped my cheek. "Where'd you go?"

"Sorry. Thinking." I offered her a grin and stepped down to the second stair. "All right, keep going."

Kiersten's hand tensed in mine, but she stepped down.

"See?" I splashed some of the water with my hand. "No big deal, super easy. The water's nice."

"Nice," she repeated with her teeth chattering. "Right, it's nice." She took the final stair, bringing the water level to her waist. Damn, she looked good in that suit. So maybe some of my past was coming back to haunt me. I was acting like a selfish ass, but I'd been wondering for weeks what she'd look like in a bathing suit. I'd wanted to see every inch of that glowing skin. I'd wanted to watch the sunlight reflect off her hair.

Couldn't a dying man at least have one last wish? Even prisoners on Death Row were given a last meal — she was mine.

"Come on." I swam backward and let the water wash over my chest. It was comfortably heated at ninety degrees, almost like a giant hot tub.

With a curse, Kiersten walked toward me, the water rising to her breasts. I knew I was acting like a complete guy, but I stared and then was suddenly so jealous of the water touching her in spots I never could that I swore and looked away.

"Wes?" Kiersten reached out and grabbed my arm. "I'm freaked, and like I said, I want to get this done as fast as possible."

"Ah, stop saying that; you'll hurt my ego."

"Fine." Her teeth chattered some more. "I'm excited—" She looked like she was walking to her death. "—to get started, so can we, just… swim?"

"Sure." I grinned. "First lesson…"

"What?"

"Float."

"I can't."

"Everyone floats."

"I don't know how."

I sighed and looked into her eyes. "Do you trust me?"

She nodded slowly.

"Okay, then lean back. Feel my hand? I won't let you drown, and it's not deep enough for that to happen in the first place; lean back and relax, think about something happy."

"I'm too terrified to think." Her body was stiff as a board as she leaned against my hand and began to float.

"Think about kissing." My hands moved from her back to her butt as I held her body in a plank position. "Think about my hands running slowly over your body until all you can do is think about what I'm going to do next."

"What are you going to do next?" Her voice was quieter, her breathing labored as she lay in my arms, trusting me.

"I'm going to devour you with my eyes. I'm going to look at every inch of skin, memorize it, store it in the little box in my head labeled *the most beautiful girl in the world*. I'm going to hold you until you're ready for me to let go, and then, when you float on your own, I'm going to keep staring, keep wanting, keep desiring, until I have to go jump into the Sound."

Her body went limp against my arms.

I let go.

She didn't move, just continued to float. "Just warn me when you let go."

"Okay." I laughed. "I'm going to let go, all right?"

She tensed and already began to sink as her body folded in half. I grabbed her before she did sink and pulled her into my arms. "Your first lesson is in fear."

"Huh?" Her hands were pressed against my chest.

"You were floating on your own for around fifteen seconds before I told you I was going to let go. The minute I said I was going to let go, you braced yourself for sinking — your mind failed; therefore, your body failed."

Kiersten made a face and looked away. "So basically, I sabotaged myself."

"Basically." I grinned, loving how she was holding her bottom lip hostage between her teeth. "You can't go into things with the mindset of already failing. Being fearful isn't necessarily a bad thing."

"Right." She clenched her eyes shut and crossed her arms. "I get what you're saying; I just don't know how to control it. Every time I see the water or a pool, I start to shake. I freak, thinking the same thing's going to happen to me that happened to my parents. Yes, I know it's illogical, but the fear is still there."

"Fear…" I uncrossed her arms and linked my fingers with hers. "Is what makes us feel alive. Fear causes our blood vessels to constrict, and then the amygdala, a tiny almond-shaped part of our brain, sends signals to our parasympathetic nervous system. The signal says, run or fight."

"I say run." Kiersten laughed humorlessly.

"Right." I tugged her closer to my body. "That's how we keep ourselves from getting eaten by wild animals. We need a fight or flight system in our body. I mean, can you imagine living in a world without fear?"

"We'd all die."

"Exactly." I chuckled. "People would be jumping off buildings thinking they could fly, so like I said, fear isn't a bad thing."

"Wait." She tried to push against my chest as I pulled her into the deep end with me. "What are you doing? I can't swim, remember?"

"I know," I whispered. "But I can."

"But—"

I ignored her. "Fear can be your ally. You can do something afraid."

"Do something afraid?"

"Yes." I swam until my legs burned, holding her up in my arms. "For example, I may be afraid of kissing you or afraid of losing you. I may be afraid that when I close my eyes, you won't be here in my arms anymore, but that doesn't mean I'm not going to hold on to you for dear life. I'm living proof that living afraid — is the way to go. You push forward, you fight the demons, you keep moving. Fear tries to paralyze you, to keep you from moving. It stops success, it stops progress — when you do things afraid, you're still accomplishing your goals, only you're doing it knowing that you are truly conquering the Everest in your life. So your parents died." I flinched. I hadn't meant to sound so blunt. But I pushed on.

"So you could die too."

Her sharp intake of breath nearly made me release her as she fought against me.

"You could die crossing the street."

Kiersten still fought me.

"You could choke on that badass turkey Melda's making."

Tears began to form in her eyes.

"You can let your fears control you, or you can control your fears. Never for one second believe the lie that you don't have a choice."

Kiersten shook in my arms, her fingers digging into my biceps like little nails getting pounded into my flesh. "What about you?" she asked in a fear-stricken voice. "What are you afraid of? What's your biggest fear?"

I should have looked away.

I should have lied.

I should have done a lot of things other than what I did.

"Dying without really living. Leaving this world knowing that the girl who makes me want to live the most — will have to do it without me."

Her eyes widened. "That's a bit heavy."

"Hey, it could be worse. I could be afraid of the water."

"Ass." She laughed and slowly started unclenching her hands from my arm.

"Move your legs," I urged. "Swimming is instinctual, just move them and allow your hands to keep your head afloat." I showed her how to tread water and then released her body from my grip.

"I'm not sinking!" she yelled and splashed around. "I'm not sinking!" Within two seconds, she was plastered against me.

"Okay." I choked as her arms wrapped around my neck. "But now I'm sinking."

"Oh." She pulled back and gripped the side of the pool with her hands. "That was—"

"—a total rush. Holy shit, it's almost like we're out here getting high." My eyes widened in excitement.

"Thank you, Wes." Damn, but I would never tire from those breathless lips as they said my name. "Thank you for not thinking I'm crazy."

"Ah, we're all a bit crazy, don't you think?"

"Yeah." She sighed. "Especially us."

"I'm going to kiss you now," I warned as my mouth collided with hers. Our tongues twisted, and I pulled her back into the water with me, floating backward as her legs wrapped around my waist. My body flared to life as her breasts pressed against my chest. Groaning in frustration, I reached for the string of her swimsuit, telling myself it was okay to be the guy I used to be, the guy that would screw her brains out without a second thought.

But I hesitated. My hand hovered over the strings as if my fingers had forgotten how to pull loose a girl's swimsuit with one hand.

"Wes?" My dad called. "You guys out here?"

I cursed and gently pushed Kiersten away, linking my hands with hers as I yelled back. "In the pool."

He rounded the corner and smiled, understanding washed over his face. "I, uh, hope I'm not interrupting anything."

"Not at all," I said too quickly.

"Right." He chuckled. "Um, I need to talk to you about something, Wes. The school called and—" He looked behind me to Kiersten. "You know, we can talk later. Why don't you kids get out and grab some hot coffee. I DVR'd the Thanksgiving Day Parade just in case you'd want to watch it."

"Yes!" Kiersten shouted from behind me. "I haven't seen the parade in years!"

"Great." Dad smiled and gave me that knowing look, the one that said, you better not screw this up with your bullshit. I smiled back, the smile every son gives to his father when he wants to remind him that he's a grown man and not a little kid anymore.

"Let's go." I grabbed Kiersten's hand and kissed it. "We can skinny dip later."

THIRTY-FOUR

Had I lost my ever-loving mind? Wes teaches me to swim, and I basically throw myself at him in his pool. Oh gosh, imagine what's going to happen when we bungee jump; I'm probably going to try to peel his clothes off as we fall.

Kiersten

I changed and went downstairs to meet Wes, but he hadn't made it down yet. It was already one in the afternoon. Melda had everything set up for dinner at four, which meant we had a few hours to ourselves. I wasn't kidding when I said I hadn't watched the parade in years. I'd always watched it with my parents, and once they died, it just seemed pointless. In fact, everything had seemed pointless. Weird how it took stepping outside of my dark, selfish little world to actually see how ridiculous my behavior had been.

Pouting hadn't brought them back.

Crying didn't make me feel better.

Hiding in my room hadn't made the pain go away.

But living — living had been my salvation, just like Wes. He was like my own personal life coach — only I was afraid I was falling too hard and fast to find my way back. I pushed away that thought — we liked each other, that was all that mattered. If I looked too far into the future, I would over-think things. After all, I was only eighteen. I didn't want to get married.

Holy crap! Was I thinking about marriage already?

See? This was why girls needed other girlfriends to reign them in. I momentarily thought about calling Lisa, but that girl was anything but the voice of reason. She'd probably drive me to Vegas if I asked her.

My finger hovered over the phone, just as I gained enough courage to dial Gabe's number, the phone lit up.

It was him.

"Hey," I answered. "I was just going to call you."

I waited on the living room couch for Wes to show up and twirled my hair in my fingers.

"Sure you were," Gabe said, laughing. "I was just calling to make sure you were still alive. I heard you went for a swim."

"How?" I gasped. "That was only forty minutes ago."

"Someone's boyfriend called to update me on the adventures of Kiersten." I could practically see Gabe's smug grin in my mind as he spoke. "And he wanted me to be the first to give you a high five for being brave."

"Swimming isn't brave," I whined. "I feel like a five-year-old."

"I wore water wings until I was fourteen," Gabe said dryly. "What you did was brave."

"Fourteen?" I repeated.

"I had a minor shark phobia."

"In a pool?"

"We aren't talking about me." Gabe changed the subject. "How goes the fairy tale, Cinderella?"

"It goes well." I sighed happily into the phone. "He's perfect, I mean, it's perfect. I feel good. Too good, almost like something bad has to happen or something, you know?"

Gabe grew really quiet.

"Gabe?"

"Yeah, I'm here." He cursed softly. "Just thinking. Look, I gotta go, but do yourself a favor? Don't over-think things. Just enjoy having the richest twenty-one-year-old in the world at your beck and call, kiss him goodnight, and savor the moments you guys have together."

"Huh?"

"You know…" Gabe cleared his throat. "Before school starts again."

"Oh right, next week, school. I almost forgot, thanks for bringing me some early Christmas cheer."

"I did work at the mall as an elf once."

"Pictures?"

"All destroyed in a tragic fire that only ended up burning that one section of my room — odd really." He laughed. "Now, go have fun; I'll see you Monday, okay?"

"Fine!"

"Oh, and don't forget, you're going shopping for a homecoming dress with Lisa. She'll freak if you forget."

"Got it."

Wes walked into the room. I hung up the phone, not even realizing I hadn't said goodbye until it was too late.

"Tattletale." I narrowed my eyes as Wes innocently lifted his hands into the air.

"I thought you needed another cheerleader on your team, that's all." His face looked a bit sunken. Dark shadows were beginning to show beneath his eyes.

"Are you feeling okay?" I asked, touching my hand to his forehead.

"Sure." His smile was tight.

"Wes," I warned. "Seriously?"

He sighed. "Fine, I don't feel one hundred percent, but the good news is we're spending the rest of the afternoon watching movies and eating, and I have nakedness to look forward to later, so there is that to live for."

"So you're basically only living for two things? Food and sex?"

"Sounds about right, though I'm only living for food… living for sex just seems so—"

"Like Gabe?" I offered.

"Touché." Wes grinned and looked at the floor, shoving his hands into his jeans pockets. "I'm not that guy anymore, Kiersten; you need to know that. Damn." He licked his lips and gave me that sexy grin I was beginning to breathe for. "I wish I still was. Then maybe I wouldn't be walking around the house in a constant state of arousal."

I felt my cheeks heat with embarrassment. With a desperate sigh, he lifted my chin with his hand and kissed my lips briefly. "I like you a lot, you know that, right?"

I nodded, not trusting myself to speak because really all I wanted to know was why he wasn't that guy anymore. Furthermore, was there something wrong with me that made me defective? Why wouldn't he want that with me? I mean, I wasn't even sure I was ready; I just wanted to know I was desirable in that way to him.

"Don't give me that look." Wes sighed. "My self-control isn't all that saintly right now. In fact, I may have to lock you in your room tonight and throw away the key. It's not for lack of wanting you." He grabbed my hands and kissed the insides of my wrists. "It's because I want you too much — I care way too damn much — so just accept the fact that it would be a bad sign if I threw you against the wall or the ground or the table. Hell, I've had that fantasy for days now. You by the turkey." He winked and wrapped his arm around my shoulders. "I want you, but it has to be right. And right now? It's too new. Get it?"

"Sure." I lied because I still hadn't gotten over the shock of me and him on a table next to the turkey. Was he insane? Shaking my head, I laughed and followed him into the media room.

"Parade." He threw a pillow at my face.

"Bring on Tom the Turkey." I held up my hand for a high five, but instead of reciprocating, he pulled me in for a scorching kiss.

"Kissing…" He sighed. "Better than a high five any day."

"And for once… Lamb agrees," I teased.

"Wolf is very pleased with Lamb's understanding of his wisdom. Now sit before Wolf pounces."

"Sitting."

"So demure. I think I like being bossy."

"Keep being bossy, and we'll see how much you like being slapped by the demure little lamb."

"And pressing play," Wes muttered.

THIRTY-FIVE

He had to go and ruin it — he had to mention Tye — he just couldn't let well enough alone... Just once, I want a normal holiday where we aren't reminded of death knocking on every damn door in our house.

Weston

"I said I don't want to talk about it," I growled, trying to push past my dad. Why was he bringing this up now? Dinner had been incredible; Melda was so excited we didn't fight at the table that she actually cried while clearing away the dishes.

It was the first Thanksgiving we had where we actually finished eating without going at each others' throats. After all, Tye had committed suicide Thanksgiving weekend.

Two years ago tomorrow, to be exact.

He'd said he had stuff to get done back on campus and drove the few miles it took to get there.

The next day we were supposed to go shopping with Melda. She was a Black Friday fanatic.

Tye was found in his room. A bottle of pills in his hand. The autopsy report came back with an insane amount of

Xanax and alcohol in his system. He'd just stopped breathing. His diaphragm unable to lift his lungs enough for him to catch a breath.

When the ambulance came, they had hoped they could save him.

He died that night at the hospital.

I hated hospitals.

"Look at me when I talk to you." My dad slammed his fist against the desk; tears welled in his eyes. "I can't lose you too!"

"I want to stay."

"Damn it, Wes!" He pinched the bridge of his nose. "One more game could kill you. You do realize that, don't you?"

"I gave her my word."

"She's a girl!" Dad all but shouted. "She'll get over it! How do you know she even likes you? Or likes anything about you other than your good looks and money? Of course, she likes you now. You've given her everything girls dream of, but what about when she finds out about your sickness? What about when she discovers you aren't on the football team anymore? What do you think will happen then? Will she stick around and hold your hand? Or go find one of your teammates to screw?"

Never in my life had I wanted to punch my father so hard.

"Don't say that about her," I fired back. "You don't know her like I do."

"Young love." My dad shook his head. "Don't you get it, Wes? It's not about her. I worry about you. I worry she's going to break your heart. I worry, I worry, I worry. I can't lose both sons." His voice broke. "I've lost everything. It would kill me to lose you too. Your focus — it needs to be on getting better, not losing yourself in her. Have you even taken your meds today?"

My last pill burned a hole the size of Texas in my pocket. I nodded jerkily and then shrugged. "I have my last pill for the weekend, and then I start the final set Monday."

Dad sighed. "Just, don't let her get in the way of your progress, son. You need to live, I can't—" His voice broke again.

"You have to come to grips with something, Dad," I said in a thick voice. "I may not live."

"No, don't say that. I refuse to believe it. The doctors said—"

"The doctors said there was a chance I'd be fine. The doctors also haven't worked with this aggressive of a tumor before. It may be too late already. Okay? Just... don't put all this pressure on me to live — when my reality may be the exact opposite. Don't get me wrong. I'll fight hard as hell to stay here as long as I can, but don't burden me with guilt — if fighting still isn't enough."

The room was blanketed in a tense silence. Then I saw my dad do something I hadn't seen him do since Tye's death. He fell into a heap on his chair and burst into tears. Shoulders shaking, the sobs coming from his mouth were heart-wrenching. My gut twisted as I made my way over to him and put my hands on his shoulders.

He gripped my hands and continued to sob. "It isn't fair."

"Cancer's rarely fair," I mumbled. "And we were never promised life would be fair."

"It should be."

"Dad." My voice croaked. "Life isn't fair, but living? Living is heaven. Living is a gift. Every gift is different — every path is different — for some reason, this is ours, and the sooner we accept it, the sooner we can stop crying and start living."

"When did you get so smart?" He laughed through his tears.

"All that damn therapy you made me go through — and sometimes, Dad, it takes going through hell to reach your heaven." I looked at the door.

"That bad, huh?"

"What?"

"You like her that much?"

"No." I swallowed. "I love her."

THIRTY-SIX

Little by little, I was beginning to live for his smiles, his touch, just anything. Heck, if he waved, my heart would still be doing somersaults.

Kiersten

"I can't believe we're doing this," I grumbled, dropping my bathing suit bottoms to the ground and clenching my eyes shut. Brave. I needed to be brave.

"I'm not stealing your virtue, so don't worry about that." Wes chuckled from the pool as he splashed around. "And I'm going to turn away while you slowly ascend the stairs. Though I'm not gonna lie, I have a very vivid imagination, so while you get into the pool, I'll be daydreaming."

"Not creepy," I joked.

"Not creepy at all. Beautiful, it's damn beautiful."

"Huh?"

"Sorry, started early," he called. "Now hurry up!"

"Shit."

"Aw, Lamb said a dirty word," Wes teased. "Stepping out of your comfort zone makes you such a bad girl."

"Okay, I'm getting in."

"Turning." I heard water splashing as I walked over to the edge and dropped my towel. The moon outlined Wes's body perfectly. His sculpted back was what every single love song was talking about — his body was what leading men fought for. Beautiful, the water lapped around his waist. I looked lower. Fantastic. Well, the water wouldn't be leaving a ton of things to the imagination if I was standing directly under the moon. Just to be safe, I walked along the edge of the pool and got in where the moon had cast a shadow. I wasn't taking any chances that Wes would see me, not that I was ashamed of my body or anything. But yeah, it was a little much, being naked in a pool with another person. It could have been Lisa, and I would have still been freaked.

The warm water felt good against my body. I was more nervous than before; everything seemed more alive, more sensitive. I slowly walked to where Wes was standing and hunched down so that the water was on my shoulders. Not only was I conquering my fear of being in the water again for the second time in one day, but I was wearing absolutely nothing.

"How's the birthday suit feel?" he asked without looking at me.

"Weird."

"You'll get used to it." He shrugged and turned. I held my breath.

"Why aren't you breathing?"

I exhaled.

"You that scared still?" he asked, concern marring his features.

"Of the water?" I looked around. "A bit. Of you? A lot."

"Want me to tell you embarrassing stories about myself so that there isn't an ounce of attraction left between us? I mean, I'll do it if I have to. I don't want to but—"

Laughing, I waited.

"Fine. When I was six, I jumped off our roof and tried to fly. I landed in the pool, so it wasn't that big of a deal, and my dad saw the whole thing. My brother dared me to do it. He also dared me to eat a fly."

"Did you?"

"What?"

"Eat a fly?"

"I ate two. He said the first one wasn't big enough, so he picked out another."

"Wow." I gripped his hand in mine, still feeling a bit nervous. "Sounds like you were picked on a bit."

"A lot. I was picked on a lot, but I'd do it all again if—" His voice cracked. "If I could have one more chance to tell him I love him."

I released his hand and pressed my fingers against his back, rubbing back and forth, trying to offer him comfort even though I didn't have the right words to say.

"It's why I wanted you to come… I mean, initially. You make me feel strong… Crazy, right? He killed himself on Black Friday — the day has double meaning for me. Sometimes I wonder if he did it on purpose. If he chose that day because it had the word black in it, or if he chose that day because it was my mom's birthday, and she had already been dead in the ground for a few years. I'll never know, I guess."

"Wow," I breathed. "Black Friday sucks for you."

He laughed. "You could say that again. Granted, it's not always on Black Friday, but the day he killed himself just happened to be that day, so regardless of if the actual date is off by a week or so — I still hate it."

"Thank you for trusting me with all of this." I pulled him in for a hug without even thinking. Our bodies may as well have erupted with heat the minute they touched. We fit. Every single part fit. I looked into his eyes and knew this was the guy — he was the one I wanted to spend my every waking moment with. He was my forever.

"Thank you for agreeing to come — and for being my girlfriend. I don't feel like I deserve you — or that I deserve this." Our fingers interlocked as he pulled me tighter against him. "Hell, I know I don't deserve this."

"Life isn't about deserving." I closed my eyes and sighed. "Aren't you the one always spouting all that wisdom?"

He grinned.

"If we wait until we're deserving, we're going to be waiting for a really long time." I shrugged. "I'd rather appreciate the fact that I'll never deserve anything — doesn't make me a bad person, just makes me all the more thankful."

"Then that's what I am," Wes whispered. "I'm thankful for you. I thank God for you. Maybe He can see me after all." He tilted his face toward the sky. "In this moment, I can believe He cares."

"Why?"

Wes looked down into my eyes. "Because He gave me you."

Breath hitched in my chest as Wes's lips grazed my cheek and then my chin, nose, eyes, and finally my lips. "Favorite Thanksgiving ever."

I sighed against his mouth. "We'll have to top it next year."

His grip tightened on my arms as he pushed me against the side of the pool, "Promise me."

"Promise you we'll do better?"

"Promise me that no matter what, you'll make Thanksgiving next year better than this year." His eyes were fierce, glowing in the moonlight. I wasn't sure what caused the sudden attitude change.

I nodded slowly. "Promise."

His grip loosened. "Sorry, I didn't mean to go all crazy on you."

"Sorry, I didn't mean to dunk you."

"Huh? You didn't—"

I pushed his head underwater and tried my best to get back to the shallow end by grabbing the side of the pool. I still wasn't a strong enough swimmer to make it on my own. So close, and then his hands came around my waist. His fingertips accidentally grazed my breasts.

I froze.

He seemed to stop breathing as he slowly turned me in his arms to face him. His hungry eyes devoured every inch of my body. I was halfway out of the water. Holy crap, what was I supposed to do?

"If I didn't want to go to heaven so damn bad..." He smiled sadly and released me. "Let's go watch a movie."

"No more skinny dipping?"

"If we skinny dip any longer, I can't make good on my promises." Wes cursed and looked away, swimming farther into the deep end.

"Oh yeah?" I put my hands on my hips, kind of digging the fact that he was having trouble with control.

"Yeah, like if you don't get out of this damn pool in five seconds, I'm going to take advantage of you against the wall, and I'd hate for your first time to be over so quick."

I blushed. And then I hightailed it out of the pool feeling all kinds of embarrassed and excited.

"Good choice!" He called after me as I grabbed my towel and went to change.

I told myself it was ridiculous to have to spend the night in Wes's arms in order to not have bad dreams, so I got ready for bed and promised myself I'd try to sleep by myself and not be such a baby.

I was just piling the throw pillows into the corner when someone knocked on my door. With one last throw, the pillows were off, and I made my way over to the door. I opened it just a crack and saw Wes, again shirtless and just in a pair of low pajama bottoms.

"Lamb?" His head tilted almost like a predator.

"Wolf," I said dryly.

"I thought you might be scared." He cleared his throat and rocked on his feet. "So I'm here to offer my cuddling services."

"Are you?" I crossed my arms and laughed. "How noble."

"I thought so." He looked down at the ground and leaned against the door frame. "Actually, I just wanted to spend the night with you... it's close to midnight, and I really... don't want to wake up alone, not on Black Friday."

I opened the door wider and let him walk in.

"Rules..." I cleared my throat. "You have to spoon."

"Let me out! Let me out!" He laughed and tried to make his way back to the door, but I stopped him and pushed against his chest.

"Promise me." I let my hands trail down his muscles and dip into his pajama pants.

He swayed toward me. "I'll promise you anything if you keep doing what you're doing."

"So weak." I shook my head.

"So attracted." He tilted my chin. "So hard — to say no to."

"So say yes." I winked over my shoulder and jumped into bed.

"Tell me, when did you become such a temptress?"

"It's the red hair." I sighed and turned on my side.

"It really is." Wes reached for my hair and twirled it around his fingers, "I'm going to miss your hair."

"'Cause I'm cutting it?" I asked.

"Nah, I'm just going to miss not having it suffocating me in the morning. You have no idea how arousing it is to wake up with your scent all over me."

I wasn't sure what to say.

"I made you uncomfortable," Wes said in a sheepish voice. "Sorry, you know how I am with censoring myself."

I tucked my hands under my head. "It's okay."

The room fell silent. Wes lay on his back, staring up at the ceiling. His breathing was even and somewhat loud. I noticed the black under his eyes again, and then I looked closer. His skin wasn't its normal golden hue; it had a pale look to it, almost like he'd been vampiring it all over town and was in need of a fix.

"Wes." I licked my lips. "Would you lie to me?"

"Huh?" He turned so quick we almost bumped heads.

"Just answer."

"No." He quickly broke eye contact.

"Are you feeling okay?"

His nostrils flared, he looked down, and then his shoulders slumped as if he was carrying the weight of the world on his shoulders. "Ask me after Homecoming."

"Huh? Why after Homecoming?"

He shrugged. "I can't lie to you, so ask me after Homecoming. Then I'll tell you."

"You'll tell me why sometimes you look healthy as a horse and other days you look like you can barely stand?"

"All of it." His voice was thick and hoarse. "I promise."

"Okay." I wasn't satisfied, not by a long shot. Maybe he had diabetes or something else like that? Heck, I knew how guys were with being sick, especially if they were anything like my Uncle. Pride was huge, and it was entirely possible he was just embarrassed about all of it.

His muscled arm came around my shoulders as he pulled me to him. "Time to spoon, Lamb."

"I've only ever spooned with you."

"Good," he whispered in my ear. "I want your firsts to be with me… that way, I can kill whoever gets you second."

"I only want firsts."

He ran his left hand over my hip. "I want that too."

"Goodnight, Wes."

"Night, my little lamb."

THIRTY-SEVEN

Time is going by way too fast — my body can feel it, my soul hates it, and my heart is breaking every damn day.

Weston

The weekend with Kiersten was at the top of my list as best weekends ever. Friday, I hadn't been in the mood to do anything except mope around. We watched movies all day and ate popcorn balls.

Saturday, we swam some more, and Sunday, I helped her put together her schedule for Spring Semester. She was still trying to pick a major. She said she wanted to pick one and have it over with — her idea was that her major should be purposeful; she wanted a purpose in her life. I couldn't blame her for that, so I just stayed silent and helped her pick the Gen Eds she would need anyway.

By the time Monday rolled around, I knew the clock was not going in my favor. I had started my new meds and hadn't dealt with that kind of nausea since starting my treatment.

Both David and James were worried, especially since I had one more football game before I was officially off the team.

She'd never seen me play.

I'd always played for the team, for the fans, for my dad, for Tye, even for myself. I'd never in my life played for a girl. It was special, and I wanted to do a good job, which meant I had to haul ass to practice when all I really wanted to do was puke and sleep. Food had completely lost its taste. In fact, it had been slowly getting worse ever since last month. Kiersten obviously didn't know, but it was like every time she ate, I tried to imagine what it tasted like. Tried to remember how turkey tasted, how sugar tasted.

Concentrating on those things just made me feel weak. I mean, how lame was it that a six foot four, two hundred twenty pound guy was upset because he couldn't taste turkey anymore?

I wiped the sweat from my forehead and did another deadlift. Tony was spotting me as usual when Coach came up behind us and took his spot.

"You up to it?" he asked as I did another lift.

"Yup." I clenched my teeth as I threw the weight down. "I've got this."

"M'kay." Coach looked away and wiped at his eyes. "And if there's anything I can do—"

"I'm not dead yet, Coach." I snapped.

"I know." His eyes watered.

Aw, shit. I put my hands on my hips and sighed, looking away from the man who'd given me my scholarship, who'd watched me play at BHS when I was a senior. We'd been to Hell and back, and I'm sure it felt to him like he was losing family. I knew that only because it felt the same way to me.

My team was my family.

They were my brothers.

I worried about them, I fought with them, I ate with them. We were a team, and I hated to think about them going on without me. I despised the fact that I wouldn't be there to offer my support when they graduated, or went to their first jobs, or possibly got the bowl game we'd been wanting since Oregon stole it from us last year.

"I'm a fighter," I finally said, my gaze never wavering as I stared Coach down. "And I'm going to win."

"Hell yes, you are." Coach stalked toward me and got right in my face. "You sure as hell will beat this thing, and you'll do me proud, you hear?"

"Loud and clear, sir." I choked on the tears burning at the back of my throat.

"Okay." He patted my back. "Good talk. Now hit the showers."

He wiped his face as he made his way back to his office and slammed the door.

"Is it just me, or is Coach a lot more emotional lately?" Tony said from behind me. I wondered how much he'd heard.

"Ah, he's just nervous about the game." I slapped Tony on the back. "You heard Coach. Hit the showers!" I yelled at my team, quite possibly for the last time. The game was tomorrow, Tuesday. And it would be my last for a while.

THIRTY-EIGHT

I want him more than anything... could a person major in Weston Michels? Because I'd for sure pick that major over kinesiology any day!

Kiersten

"**J**ust put on the damn shirt." Gabe thrust it into my face again and sighed. "We're going to be late."

I felt my face flush with embarrassment as I stomped over to my room and threw on the shirt. *Team Wes* had been printed in red across the front, surrounded by giant hearts. Why had Gabe done that? I still didn't get why I had to wear it. But Gabe had insisted, saying it was Homecoming tradition and that it would make Wes proud to see me wearing something with his name on it. He said it would give him courage. I was still stuck on the idea that a guy like Wes would need courage to do anything, but I left it alone. Besides, it seemed Gabe was already irritated with me though I didn't know why.

"Better?" I walked out of the room and did a quick turn. I wore a pair of cute Nike shoes, ripped jeans, and the t-shirt.

My hair was in a ponytail, and I had paint on my face with Wes's number on it — thirty-two in Husky purple and gold.

"Awesome." Gabe pumped his fist. "See? Was that so hard?"

"Listening to you?" I jutted out my hip. "Always hard."

"Love you too." Gabe rolled his eyes. "Now grab your shit; we gotta go." He slapped my butt and called for his cousin. "Get your ass out here, Lisa, or so help me I'll—"

"Coming!" She bounded out of her room. Since Gabe was taking a timeout from all the crazy girls, he'd agreed to take Lisa to the game, only if she behaved and didn't go home with some psycho dude. She must have had a more checkered past than I realized because he always seemed super concerned about her and guys.

I checked my phone. Wes would be warming up still. I sent him a text anyway.

Go Thirty-Two!

"Let's go!" I ran to the door, giddy with excitement. I'd never been to a college game before, and honestly, I'd known Wes was popular — I mean, look at him. But the fact that he was the star quarterback at a school like University of Washington? Yeah, that was some crazy stuff. Gabe said ESPN was covering the game because they were playing the Cougars. Huge rivalry. Apparently, they still hadn't let go of that whole Rose Bowl fiasco all those years ago — at least according to Gabe.

We followed the crowds to the stadium. Electricity buzzed in the air. Cameras and people were everywhere. It was overwhelming, to say the least. I hadn't expected it to be like that. Lights blinded me, and suddenly I was extremely anxious for Wes. He played like this all the time? How did he not have a nervous breakdown?

Gabe grabbed my hand and walked me to our seats. Wes had secured seats for us really close to the field so we could see the players. We were still in the student section, but it was better than nothing.

"There he is!" Lisa screamed and pointed at the field as Wes threw a football back and forth with some other guy.

"Good Lord, you've done good with that man." Lisa shook her head and whistled. "He's freaking gorgeous. Tell me what he kisses like, please, Kiersten! I beg you!" She grabbed my shirt and pulled me against her.

"And I think I'm going to sit between you guys." Gabe moved to sit in the middle while Lisa stuck out her tongue.

"Pardon my cousin." Gabe sighed. "She's been single for way too long."

"Wonder whose fault that is," she sang.

"Protecting your reputation," he fired back.

I laughed and patted Gabe's arm. "Thanks for making me wear the shirt."

Gabe gave a jerky nod and pointed at Wes. "Look, he's watching us. Hurry and stand so he can see your shirt."

I stood and pointed at the middle of my shirt, where there were hearts and his number.

He probably should have told the guy he was playing catch with that he wasn't paying attention because the football hit him in the chest.

"Epic." Gabe laughed. "Do yourself a favor, Kiersten, just sit throughout the entire game. Wouldn't want him getting a concussion."

I bit my lip to keep from smiling like a lunatic — it didn't work. I was gone, done for, I was his. And I wanted everyone to know it.

The announcer came on the loudspeaker as the players lined up.

By the time the color guard played the National Anthem, I was an absolute nervous wreck. I'd picked off every last bit of my nail polish and was starting in on biting the nails completely off when Gabe grabbed my right hand and put it under his leg, so he was sitting on it.

"Seriously, you're making me nervous, and I have to stay sober tonight, so for the love of God, stop fidgeting!" He glared.

"Fine." I took a few deep breaths and concentrated on the players as they ran out onto the field. I knew football. I mean, not super well, but I knew enough to know what was going on. The team kicked, they returned, and then when it was time for the offense to go out, Wes would run out, get some plays done and win the game. End of story.

The team kicked, and with that, my heart soared. How was I ever going to make it through more than one game with Wes playing out there? My hand fidgeted under Gabe's leg.

He swore and reached into his pocket and thrust a stick of gum in my face. "Chew. It'll help, promise."

I greedily took the gum and began chewing like my life depended on it.

"Right." Gabe took my trash. "Try not to bite your tongue off. Wes will never forgive me if you aren't in shape for kissing."

I elbowed him but didn't take my eyes off the game. The offense ran out. Wes turned quickly and waved in my direction.

He was fine. He looked fine. Everything was going to be fine.

THIRTY-NINE

I knew something was wrong when the vision blurred in my right eye. I shook it off and pressed on. I had to win. For some reason, I was envisioning the game as my battle with cancer; if I lost, I lost everything. I had to win. I had to.

Weston

I shook my head again, the blurriness cleared from my eyes. The medication was causing way more side effects than I imagined. I met the guys in the huddle and called the play. It was a trick play, one that was kind of risky for the beginning of a game, but we wanted to throw the Cougars off. Damn, I hated the Cougars; all Huskies did. I even hated their colors.

"Ready? Break!" I ran to the center and called, "Red twenty-nine, left, Red twenty-nine left, hut, hut!"

The football sailed into my hands. I dropped back as if I was throwing long and then did a fake throw to the right while running to the left. Tony blocked ahead of me, five yards… ten… fifteen. A lineman tried grabbing my ankle, but I jumped over him and ran all the way to the twenty-yard line.

"Good run!" Tony slapped my back. My vision blurred; this time, it stayed. Shit and double shit. I tried shaking my head, but it wouldn't clear. I could see figures, but they were blurry. Everything was blurry, but I could still see the ball, and my breathing was normal. I was going to keep playing. I had to.

We scored easily, and so began the hardest game of my life.

Each time I shook my head, the vision got worse. By the time the fourth quarter was rolling around, I felt like I had drunk a whole bottle of tequila. My vision wasn't clear, and my balance was so terrible that I had to focus on each step I took.

We were ahead by so much that Coach took me out to give the second-string quarterback some experience. I think he saw that I was fading. I sat on the bench and pretended to be really into the game, which was hard considering all I could think about were the spots now invading my vision. Not good. It felt like I had a migraine coming on, but I couldn't be sure. Maybe I had overdone it. The good news was the game was already over, so it didn't matter anymore.

I just wanted to lie down with a cold compress against my head — well, I wanted that and to hold Kiersten, but I knew if she saw me like this, she would know what was wrong. We had a Homecoming party to go to tonight — I wasn't sure I would make it.

I took another few sips of water and closed my eyes, hoping the rest would make it better.

Another few minutes went by, and Coach came up beside me and slapped me on the shoulder. "You want to do one last play?"

I knew what he was asking.

One last play before my bleak future went black. His guess was as good as mine as to if I'd live to see a football again. Black spots or no black spots, I needed to do this.

I stood on shaky legs and made my way out onto the field amidst the screams from the fans. Damn, I'd miss it. I'd miss the feel of running out onto the field, the buzz of excitement.

With a sigh, I turned and saw Kiersten on her feet yelling. I blinked, my vision returned just enough for me to see her waving frantically. Her shirt had a heart on it. Hell, she had no idea the encouragement that gave me, but Gabe did. I blew her a kiss then nodded my head to him.

I could have sworn he yelled, "Give 'em hell!"

Laughing, I shakily made my way to the huddle. We'd already won, so now it was time to show off. I called a fake play in order to get the other team offsides and decided to do the exact same trick play Boise State had done in the Fiesta Bowl a few years back.

As I suspected, the team fell for it, gaining us five yards. My heart thundered in my chest. Everything felt heavy as if someone had put a piano on top of me. I took a few deep breaths and called the play.

"Baby blue, baby blue, BSU, hut!" When I fell back, I stumbled, tripped, or something. I wasn't really sure, but that pause was enough for me to see a lineman heading straight for me. I was too late. My vision blurred, then went completely black as I felt myself falling backward against the ground.

The last thing I remembered was thinking I never told her I loved her, and that sucked because she needed to know — I would die, was probably dying, and the last thought in my mind, the last word that blew across my lips was "Kiersten."

FORTY

Can a person's heart shatter in their chest?
Because I think mine just did...

Kiersten

"Something's wrong." Gabe clenched my hand in his and watched as Wes stumbled out onto the field. He ran like he was drunk; maybe he was just trying to show off and be funny.

I shrugged. "He wouldn't go out there if something was wrong."

Gabe snorted. "Then you don't know how guys work." He waved his hands above his head, trying to gain the coach's attention. "Shit!" He pushed me toward the chairs and jumped onto the field, running to the coach. I was still trying to figure out what the hell his problem was when I saw it.

The ball fell from Wes's hands. He wavered on his feet and collapsed onto the field.

I could have sworn the entire stadium fell into silence as I

233

screamed. Lisa held me in her arms while frantically looking at Gabe, who was cussing out the coach.

The coach ran toward the field, players looked at each other in confusion. And I knew in that moment that Wes had lied.

It wasn't diabetes.

It couldn't be.

Something was wrong, and he hadn't told me. Nobody just passed out on the field like that. He was strong, wasn't he? He was healthy, right?

I held my breath as doctors rushed onto the field. I prayed. I prayed hard that Wes would move, that I would see his fingers drum onto the grass, or that he would jump into the air and start laughing like it was some giant joke. I didn't realize I was crying until Lisa handed me a tissue from her purse.

"He's okay, right?" I asked in a hoarse voice. "Right? He's just tired? Or dehydrated?"

"Sure." Lisa gripped my hand in hers.

The sound of an ambulance almost killed me.

I couldn't do this. I couldn't just stand there and wait. I ran. I ran as fast as I could and jumped over the barrier, so I was on the field with Gabe. He intercepted me in his arms as I ran for Wes. And then another set of arms braced me.

I turned and cried.

I cried into Randy Michels's chest like he was my dad like he was my lifeline. I clung on to him with everything I had. The funny part? He held me right back as if I was his lifeline too.

"He'll be okay," Randy whispered. "He's a fighter, okay? He's a fighter, don't you forget it!" He nodded as his Adam's apple bobbed against my face. "He's not like his brother, God rest his soul. Wes is strong. He's like his mom." Randy sighed.

"Come on, I'll take you to the hospital."

I gripped Randy's hand on one side of me, and Gabe's on the other as cameras went off.

Wanting to yell, I kept my head down as we made our way off the field, amidst the flashes of cameras and yelling from the fans. They wanted to know what was wrong. They wanted to know all the things I wanted to know. I just didn't have the answers.

My body went into a state of shock on the way to the hospital. I couldn't stop shaking. I was pissed that it seemed that Gabe knew what was going on, but I didn't. Even Randy seemed like he had expected Wes to pass out. What kind of father expects his son to pass out on the field?

"Come on." Gabe tucked me under his arm, and we made our way to the private wing of the University Hospital.

"Is he stable?" Randy asked once we reached the room the nurse had directed us toward. The nurse paused and lowered her clipboard.

Her eyes flickered to mine before returning to Randy's.

"Family," he said. "They're family."

"Right." Her eyes flickered between us before she answered. "He's stable but had a very dangerous reaction with his last group of medications. As you know, they're trial basis only; there was no way for us to know he would have that type of reaction. Luckily, he was in a public place, so the minute he blacked out, he was able to get help. Had he been in his room or even—"

"That's enough," Randy interrupted with a wave of his hand. "We'd like to see him now."

"But—"

"Now," Randy said smoothly. "He needs his family."

"Yes, sir." She ducked out of the way and walked briskly down the hall, her clipboard tucked firmly under her arm.

I hated that his name was already on the door. I hated that I was in a hospital. Pausing in the middle of the doorway, I asked in a small voice, "What don't I know?"

Randy swallowed and looked to Gabe.

Why the hell would he look at Gabe?

With a curse, Gabe licked his lips and nodded into the room. "Let him tell you. I refuse to be the guy to bring that kind of news."

"That kind of news," I repeated over and over again in my head. What did that even mean? My heart clenched. My stomach felt like it was in a billion knots, yet I walked farther into the room.

Wes was hooked up to an IV and a heart monitor, but other than that, he looked normal, healthy even.

His eyes flickered open. He groaned and asked, "Did we win?"

"By a lot, man." Gabe laughed. "Though we could have done without the theatrics."

"Theatrics?" he asked, his voice kind of slurring. "Holy shit! Kiersten! Where is she? I have to tell her. I have to…" His voice died off when I stepped out from behind Gabe. Tears streamed down my face, most likely ruining the paint. I watched his face fall.

"Give us a minute," he whispered.

His dad nodded at me, then kissed Wes on the forehead and walked out with Gabe, leaving us in a crazy, tense silence.

"So," I said in a shaky voice. "It's after Homecoming."

Wes didn't reply.

I didn't care. I was just glad he was breathing. I moved to

the side of his bed and sat, folding my hands in my lap. "You promised you'd tell me everything. No more lies, no more omissions."

With a shudder, I looked into his eyes. They pooled with tears as he blinked a few times and then closed them. "I'm sick."

"Figured that." I bit my lip. "How sick?"

"People always ask that you know?" He chuckled. "How sick are you? On a scale of one to ten, will you die? Are you nauseated? Rate the nausea." He laughed again. "Lamb... the wolf is really sick."

"As in, the wolf got shot, and it's only a flesh wound?" I asked, hopefully.

"Monty Python." He actually laughed. "Classic, and to answer your question, probably more than a flesh wound."

"Oh." I bit my lip to keep from crying, but the tears came anyway. Didn't he know? I was his. He was mine. How could God do this to me? How could he take the one thing I could count on? I kept rubbing my hands together — most likely rubbing them raw until Wes grabbed them and pulled me down to his side, caressing my face with his fingers.

"I have cancer."

The ground fell out beneath me.

Drowning.

I was drowning like I'd always feared — only this time it wasn't in water, it was in air. I couldn't breathe, I couldn't think. That one word: *cancer*. The word every person feared. That word had the power to destroy a person, only cancer never destroyed in an instant. It was always slow. It always tortured. My heart felt like it stopped beating. I tried to suck in a breath, but nothing would come.

"Hey, hey." Wes grasped my head against his chest and sighed. "You're fine. It's fine. It's just a shock. You're okay. Just breathe."

Apparently, my body needed permission from him to do something that simple — to breathe. I took in a few soothing breaths and then asked the inevitable.

"Will you get better?"

"I want to," Wes said against my hair. And then I gasped. Everything made sense. His obsession with my hair, all his cryptic talk about not being here or about giving me as much time as he had.

I fell into a sob over his chest. I couldn't control myself. "No, No, No." I slammed my fist into the mattress as he held me tight. "You have more time than that, Wes. Damn it! You have more time! Promise me! Promise me this isn't goodbye! Promise me, Wes, Promise!"

Arms came around me; they weren't Wes's. I collapsed onto the floor in those arms.

I noticed tattoos first — Gabe. It was Gabe.

"Hold it together," he whispered in my ear. "And let him talk. I'll be ready to take you home in a few, okay?"

I nodded. I wasn't going home. I wasn't freaking leaving Wes's side. But I nodded anyway.

"You can't die," I said in a shaky voice.

Wes smiled. "I don't want to."

"Why did you collapse?"

He patted the mattress, and I sat again, trying to keep myself from going into hysterics.

"My dad's rich, what can I say? It's my last week of experimental drugs before I go in for surgery."

My head jerked up. "Surgery?"

238

"Yeah, to remove the tumor."

"Well, where is it?" This was good, right? If they removed it, the cancer would be gone!

"Wrapped around my heart."

"Oh, God." I closed my eyes as more tears rolled down my cheeks, "Do they, um…" I sniffled. "Do they think they can get it all?"

Wes leaned forward and wiped some of the tears from my cheeks with his thumbs. "Aw little lamb, don't cry." He held my hand and squeezed it. How could he have a tumor when he looked fine? "I'm about fifty-fifty at this point. They don't know if they can get it all, but because it's so close to my heart, they get too close, and they could kill me. They don't get it all, and I die anyway."

I couldn't trust myself to speak, so I just stared into his crystal blue eyes and prayed the nightmare would vanish.

"Will you…" Wes licked his lips and fidgeted with my hands. "Will you stay with me?"

"Nightmares?" I tried to joke, but the tears kept streaming.

"Yeah," he choked. "Nightmares. I kind of need a knight in shining armor to chase them away."

"I'll fight them," I whispered. "I'll protect you, slay the dragon, and wait for you in the castle."

"Promise?" He smiled, his eyes full of tears.

"With my whole heart."

"I love your heart." He sighed against my head.

"Hearts and hair, huh?" I placed my hand over his chest.

"Hearts and hair," he repeated. "Just do me a favor."

"Anything," I whispered.

"No matter what happens over the next few days, promise me you'll finish the list."

"Wes—"

"Promise me," he said sternly.

I closed my eyes as warm tears began to fall all over again. "I promise."

"Good." He exhaled. "Good."

FORTY-ONE

I held her tight all night. Later on, when Gabe came in, I told him I was keeping her. With a smirk, he told me he'd return with some fresh clothes. A year ago, I wouldn't have picked him out of a crowd — now it felt like he was my best friend. And I owed it all to the girl sleeping in my arms.

Weston

I didn't have any nightmares, and by five in the morning, when the nurse checked on me again. I felt back to my old self.

Except for the fact that they moved the surgery forward. It was going to happen in less than five days. Which meant my time with Kiersten was now severely limited. In six days I could be dead, and if I wasn't dead, I'd either be in a coma or be sent home to die. I told Gabe I'd fight, and I wanted to, but it was hard to be optimistic, so damn hard.

I prayed over and over again that God would spare me, not because I cared that much about my own life — but because I cared about hers.

Sleep wasn't happening, so by the time Gabe stopped by with a duffel bag, I was wide-eyed and ready for coffee — anything but those damn pills they kept forcing down me.

"Sleeping still?" Gabe whispered when he walked in.

"Like the dead."

"Not funny, man." Gabe's voice hitched as he took a seat and put his head in his hands. "So not funny."

"Too soon?" I laughed.

"I can't…" Gabe licked his lips and looked at me. "There are others more deserving of cancer, you know? That's what gets me. Why does God allow people like you—? People, who have such a bright future — why do you get cancer when mass murderers live their lives in jail getting to watch free HBO? I don't get it."

"I don't know, man." I sighed. "I can't explain it. I guess that's just what happens when we live. Nobody is promised anything. That's why life's so precious."

"It should have been me," Gabe whispered, so I almost couldn't hear him.

"Gabe?"

"What?" He snorted. "Do you even realize what type of life I've led? The drugs? Sex? Girls? Stealing to get high? Shit, man, it should have been me. I would…" He choked on his words and looked away. "I would take your place. I just want you to know. If God told me that was my penance for living the shitty life I've lived, I'd take your place. I asked Him, hell, I begged last night, and you know what? Nothing. Silence."

"So live a better life," I snapped. "Do better. Be Better. Don't let my life be wasted. If I need to be sacrificed in order for you to get that, then that's fine. Just don't let it destroy you; let it renew you."

Gabe sniffed. I could tell he was minutes away from losing it. Hell, I'd been that way all night. It hurt like hell to keep the tears in, to stay strong when the love of my life was lying against me crying in her sleep.

"How's my favorite patient?" The nurse walked into the room and grabbed the clipboard. "You ready for your MRI?"

No. Hell, no. I didn't want to know the truth. So I'd asked them not to tell me. If I was going to die, I didn't want to know. I didn't want to go into surgery with the mindset of defeat.

"Sure, let me just wake Sleeping Beauty."

Gabe jumped to his feet. "I'll just be outside. I'm sure she'll be hungry."

"Gabe," I called after him.

He turned. "Yeah?"

"I do have one favor to ask."

"Anything."

"I need you to do something for my girl." I smiled and licked my lips. "She's going to be pissed, but promise me you'll do it."

Gabe laughed. "I like the idea already."

"I'll text you the details later. I have it set up for tomorrow, okay?"

"Sounds good." Gabe waved and walked off as I leaned down and kissed Kiersten's lips.

"Mmm," she moaned.

I kissed her lips again. Her eyes fluttered open. "Tell me it was a bad dream, Wes."

"Not a bad dream, just not my favorite." I brushed the hair from her face and closed my eyes as it ran through my fingers. "Now, as much as I love having you plastered against me, that nice nurse standing over there needs to take me for my MRI."

"Oh." Kiersten jumped to her feet, a little unsteady at first, and then shoved her hands into the pockets of her jeans. "I probably look like a mess anyway. I should go get a shower."

"Gabe has stuff for you." I nodded to the door. "My dad has a suite in his own private part of the hospital. You and Gabe can sleep there and take showers, all right? I'm assuming you want to be here and—"

"I'm not leaving your side," she vowed.

That was what I'd been afraid of. I would be the one leaving, and she — she would stay.

"All right." I yawned and gave her a wink. "I'll be done in a bit, and then we can talk all about how I'm the worst boyfriend in the world for missing the Homecoming party."

She smiled at that and walked out of the room.

"Beautiful girlfriend."

I looked at the nurse, not caring that she was probably going to think I was crazy, and said, "I would make her my wife if I could."

The nurse smiled and patted my arm. "Don't give up yet. Sometimes when we think God has written *The End*, what he really means is *The Beginning*."

The MRI scared the hell out of me. I always hated them but wasn't given much of a choice in this instance. Instead of concentrating on not moving — I thought about Kiersten. I imagined what she would look like when she was thirty. Would her smile still be the same? Would her belly be swollen with a child? Damn, but I wanted the child to be mine. I bit down hard on my lip. I had to stay still; my fists wanted to clench. I wanted to yell. My visions went on fast forward to Kiersten as an old woman sitting on the porch holding her husband's hand. I wasn't sure why I was torturing myself. Hell, I'd known her for three months, but it wasn't that instant love thing that had been a part of all my teenage and college years. I knew it was real. Maybe that was God's final gift to me — true love.

Before I knew it, the MRI was over, and my face was wet with tears. The minute I could move, I wiped the wetness from my face so nobody would notice. The last time I cried was when Tye died. Funny, how death really brings it out in people. Three months ago, I was ready. Three months ago, I had accepted my fate. But now? Now I wanted more than anything to be a part of Kiersten's story, not just a chapter, but the entire damn book. I just wasn't sure what the plan was. All I knew is it was out of my control. Maybe that was the scariest thing. In life, we always have some measure of control, whether it be over our emotions or choices, but when it comes to cancer? The only thing you can control is how you respond to it.

"How are you feeling?" that same nurse asked. She had bright blond hair, almost translucent. Her skin was a pale white, but she didn't look washed out. She was really pretty, though I couldn't tell how old she was. Maybe thirty? Forty? I must have looked confused because she put her warm hand to my forehead. "Are you feeling ill?"

"No, sorry." I laughed. "I just, I know this sounds strange, but I can't tell how old you are."

Her smile brightened. "We're as old as we feel, right?"

"Right." And I felt hella old. Especially after that morning's round of medications. At least I didn't have to swallow anything anymore. Nah, they just pumped all those fun drugs directly into my veins. Lucky me.

"Weston." Her voice was crisp. "It's going to be okay." She grabbed my hand and patted it.

I looked at her name tag, *Angela*. It fit. She seemed more angel than nurse anyway.

"Thanks, Angela."

She looked at me in confusion.

I pointed to the name tag.

She laughed. "Brilliant college boys."

"What can I say?" I grinned as she helped me back to my bed.

Forty-one or forty-five. I was going to stick with that. She was probably the same age as my mom would have been before her untimely death. She'd had blond hair too. It was probably why I was acting like a lunatic. I wondered if the drugs did that to me, made me more emotional than normal.

"Sleep," Angela ordered upon returning me to my room. "And I'll be sure to wake you when your future wife arrives." She winked.

I couldn't trust myself to talk. Although I appreciated the nurse's optimism, it fell on deaf ears. I was already starting to feel the cold seep into my limbs — as if death was coming for me, and there was nothing I could do but wait for its all-consuming presence.

"God…" I choked on the word. "I know we haven't talked much in the past few years. Hell, I told you I hated you when Tye took his own life." I cursed again and pinched the bridge of my nose. "I don't even care about myself anymore, just promise me she'll be okay. If I don't make it… if you take me, just let Kiersten be okay. She can't go down that road — I don't care if you have to punish me, God. If she's going to suffer, give me her pain instead. If her heart's going to break, break mine for hers. Please, God… please." The drugs Angela had given me started to kick in; I fell into a dreamless sleep with that prayer repeating over and over again in my head.

FORTY-TWO

Three months ago I wouldn't have been strong enough to go through this. Now? Now I felt like The Hulk — I'd hold his hand through it, we'd walk through the battle together, and in the end, we'd still be holding hands.

Kiersten

"**S**hould I be worried that you haven't said one word since we've gotten in the car?" Gabe asked.

I shook my head. "Nah, just thinking."

"Right, women and thinking. That never causes any problems for the human race."

"Hilarious." I rolled my eyes and grabbed his hand. "Gabe?"

"Yeah." He clenched my hand.

"Thank you."

"Just doing my friendship duties. Think of it as a penance for my many sins." He laughed. I could tell he was trying to make light of what he was doing. I didn't know why it was so necessary that he constantly put himself down. But there it was.

"Above and beyond friendship." I squeezed his hand and released it. "Though I am curious. Where are we going? I kind of want to be there when Wes wakes up."

Gabe grinned. "Don't you worry your pretty little head. Wes had this all planned out for you guys. Actually, the plan was for me and Lisa to come too. But it's better this way. Wes did tell me I had to video you though."

"Video me?" I repeated, dread and fear mixed in my voice. "Video what exactly?"

Gabe just kept grinning.

About thirty minutes later, we were pulling up to an old Bridge North of Seattle.

"Time to shine!" Gabe clapped his hands and nodded his head. "This is going to be epic."

"I have a bad feeling."

"No punking out. You're doing this for Wes." Gabe pointed at me and then stalked over to the bridge where a few people were setting some sort of contraption up.

Oh no. Oh no, no, no.

"Kiersten," Gabe said. "Meet the crew from Seattle Bungee. They're going to be the ones making sure all the safety stuff is in order, so you don't go splat."

"How reassuring," I mumbled dryly.

"No worries!" A guy who appeared even younger than me laughed and slapped me on the back. "We do this all time. It's our job. Haven't lost one yet, though one chick did puke. But hey, as long as you face down, you'll be fine."

Palms sweating, I gave him a jerky nod.

Harnesses were passed out, along with helmets and carabineers. Oh, my gosh! Was I really going to do this? Shaking, I let the crew fasten my harness, and then they connected me to Gabe. I was trembling so much that my lips were quivering. I hated heights. I was terrified of them almost as much as water. Why the hell had I written this on my stupid list? I closed my eyes, refusing to look over the edge.

"Look at me," Gabe commanded.

I opened my eyes as he wrapped his arms around me.

"Wes wanted me to tell you something." Gabe's eyes welled with tears. "He said that no matter what obstacle you face…" His voice shook. "No matter how afraid you are — you can still make the choice to fight. You can still make the choice to walk through the fire — he said to do it afraid."

I nodded, not trusting myself to speak as my throat was so thick with emotion it was hard to breathe.

"He said he's not giving up — and neither should you."

"I won't," I vowed. "I won't give up."

"That's my girl." Gabe kissed my cheek. Funny how one guy had ended up being my soul mate, while the other ended up being my best friend in the whole world.

"One…" Gabe whispered, "Two…"

I clutched his body so tight I couldn't breathe.

"Three."

We fell over the side of the bridge, weightless. Completely weightless. I wasn't even sure I was screaming, my mouth was open, and then the bungee bounced. It held us, and we fell again.

Then the funniest thing happened.

I started laughing.

Then crying.

Then laughing again.

I'd done it afraid. I'd conquered my fear, and all because Wes believed in me enough to push me — just like I was going to push him. He didn't want me to go into that dark place — never again. And I wasn't going to let him either.

"Thank you," I whispered into Gabe's ear as we were jerked

back up by the crew.

Gabe held my face between his hands. "What you two have — it's a once in a lifetime — you fight for him, sweetheart. Fight for him with every last breath. No regrets, okay?"

"Okay."

I laughed when Gabe handed over his phone to Wes. So apparently, I had screamed — it sounded horrific, and I had to laugh. Poor Gabe, he was probably going to have ringing in his ears for days.

"Classic." Wes laughed and then started coughing, I went to touch his arm, and he grinned. "Medicine makes me feel like shit, no worries, I'm fine."

"Gabe, can you uh—"

"Lisa just texted anyway. She's lost in the hospital, if I don't find her, she's going to hit on one of the doctors, and we really don't want to see the ramifications of that." With a salute, he left the room.

"I did it." I grinned.

Wes pulled me to his chest. I tucked my legs onto the hospital bed and laid my head against where his heart was beating. Funny, I could hear it; it sounded healthy, strong. I placed my hand there and started tapping.

"What are you doing?"

I lifted my head and gave Wes a weak smile. "Oh, just keeping our time."

His mouth found mine, and then I was straddling him, throwing off my jacket to a heap on the floor. Wes reached around my neck and pulled me closer to him. He was weak from the medication, but everything about him felt so alive still, so warm.

"You're going to fight this," I said against his lips.

He sighed and kissed me hard. "I am fighting it."

"Listen to me." I pulled back and gripped his face with my hands. "No giving up. I won't give up on you, so don't you give up on you. Okay? This is not the end."

Wes cursed. "I need you to be prepared that if it—"

"Nope," I interrupted as I kissed his cheek. "I'm not even going there. You know why?"

"Why?"

"Someone brilliant once told me that when you tell yourself you can't do something, or even entertain the possibility, the body starts giving into defeat. It's weak like that. The mind tells you that you may not make it, so you start to sink—"

"Hmm, sounds familiar."

"I started sinking," I explained, rubbing his cheeks with my thumbs. "I sank because I told myself I was drowning."

"I'm not drowning."

"And you aren't sinking." I kissed his mouth. "You're floating, just like I floated. You just have to stay above water a little bit longer than most people, but I promise the end will be worth it."

"Is there skinny-dipping in the end?" Wes tilted his head.

I threw my head back and laughed. It felt good to joke with him. "Absolutely. Lots and lots of skinny-dipping."

"My favorite." His lips were warm against my neck. I arched back as he trailed kisses down the side of my jaw.

I collapsed onto him and kissed him as hard as I could. We fell asleep talking and kissing. Every time I woke up, I kissed him again, and every time I fell asleep, it was to him kissing my hair, my neck, telling me stories.

Later Lisa and Gabe came into the room; we decided that the best way to not dwell on the future was to occupy ourselves. First, we played BS, then we watched a few Christmas movies, and ate popcorn. Lisa fell asleep first, then Gabe, and then me. The last thing I remembered before my eyes fanned closed was that the nurse was going to have a field day when she walked into our room. Gabe was stretched out in a chair, Lisa was lying on the small bed for family, and I was sprawled out on top of Wes.

I fell asleep with a smile on my lips. Friends. Best friends. I had them, and I had Wes. I tapped the rhythm of his heart with my fingers, allowing the cadence to put me into a deep sleep.

FORTY-THREE

Most people die without experiencing even half of what I have in the past few months. Incredible. I have an incredible life. I woke up feeling thankful. Even with the cancer. I woke up feeling grateful.

Weston

I laughed when Kiersten moaned in my arms. It was time for my last dose of medication. They wanted to do one last cocktail before I went in for surgery the next day.

"How are you feeling?" Angela asked as she inserted the clear liquid into my IV bag.

"Like a rock star," I lied. I felt nauseated and dizzy.

Angela laughed. "You look healthy, strong." With a grin, she pulled out her stethoscope and pressed it to my chest. "Good heartbeat."

It was all the same, but for some reason, she gave me more hope. Her eyebrows drew together, and then she removed the stethoscope and placed her hands on my chest. She closed her eyes, and I could have sworn she started crying.

Awesome, so now I was hallucinating from the medication.

My tongue felt thick in my mouth. I pointed to my

throat, and she immediately removed her hands and dropped something else into my IV. The thickness dissipated.

"Anaphylaxis." She shrugged. "These drugs tend to do that, but now that you have epinephrine in your system, you'll be able to take them."

"Epi—what?"

"Fancy word for anti-allergy meds." She winked. "And sorry about that. It's just the craziest thing. Your heart... its rhythm is stronger than it was yesterday, that's why I pressed my hand against your chest. Strange, really." She shrugged. "At any rate, congratulations, Weston. This is your last dose of medication."

"I don't like the word *last*."

Angela smiled warmly. "Remember what I said, sometimes the end is the beginning."

"Thanks, Angela."

With a final nod, she walked out the door.

I stared at Kiersten's hair, watched as it wound itself around my fingers. Flecks of gold shone through the strands. I closed my eyes and lifted it to my lips, feeling the silkiness against my skin.

"You being creepy and smelling my hair again," Kiersten said in a groggy voice.

"Not creepy," I argued.

"Very creepy," Gabe said from the chair. "I watched the whole thing, and I am sufficiently creeped out."

"It's romantic, damn it!" Lisa all but shouted.

"So what? You guys were all awake while the nurse gave me my drugs and decided to fake sleep?"

"Nurse?" Gabe looked around the room. "Where?"

"She was just here." I pointed to my IV; the liquid was still seeping into my body, stinging as it made its progress around my veins.

"Weird." Lisa scratched her head. "I didn't see anyone, then again—"

"—then again," Gabe interrupted. "You slept through Avengers twice. We can't really trust your judgment on being perceptive or knowing when things are exploding in front of your face."

"Thanks, cousin." Lisa threw her jacket at his face. "So…" She turned to me and Kiersten. "What are we going to do today?"

"I don't know, Brain, what do you want to do?"

"Pinky! Today, we're going to take over the world!" Kiersten shouted from my arms.

Gabe started laughing so hard I thought he was going to fall out of his chair.

I choked on my own laughter while Lisa just stared at all of us like we'd completely lost it.

"You know, from Pinky and The Brain?" Gabe swatted her. "Seriously, what type of childhood did you have?"

"One without cartoons." Lisa shrugged.

"Well, that settles it then." I rubbed my hands together. "Pinky and The Brain Marathon!"

"How do we even get our hands on those episodes?" Kiersten pushed to a sitting position.

"YouTube." I shrugged. "And just in case you forgot, my dad is Randy Michels. Nothing a few phone calls can't take care of."

Kiersten rolled her eyes. "Fine, but I'm going to go shower before we take over the world."

"Me too." Lisa jumped up.

"Me too?" I asked.

Kiersten swatted me. "No nakedness until after your surgery."

"Ah, and here I thought you wanted to make me happy." I pretended to be sad while Gabe gave me the thumbs up.

"Once a player…" Lisa said hopelessly into the air.

"See you in a bit, boys." Kiersten grabbed Lisa's hand as they walked out of the room, leaving me and Gabe alone.

"Why were we never friends?" I asked after a few minutes of silence.

Gabe laughed. "Well, for starters. I don't do sports, and you always had an entourage of people following you, which I'm guessing now had more to do with the cancer than anything else."

"Yup." I crossed my arms. "One was my shrink, the other was a bodyguard from when I was a kid — both were concerned that if I was left to my own devices, I'd forget to take meds or off myself like my brother did."

"Why an RA?" Gabe asked.

"He died." I licked my lips. "His damn RA said he'd been suspicious of Tye for a while. He said Tye never participated in any activities and was often locked up in his room. But he didn't tell anyone — didn't think it was any of his business. I kept thinking that if maybe I was an RA, I could help save some freshman." I laughed. "Didn't expect to fall in love with one."

Gabe joined in the laughter. "Love is never expected."

"What about you?"

"Are we really having this discussion?" Gabe scratched the back of his head and looked out the window.

"I guess we are."

"I don't do love… I don't do relationships, not anymore."

"Bad experience?"

"You could say that." Gabe bit off a curse. Then he huffed out a long breath. "But that doesn't mean I can't recognize it when it stares me in the face. She loves you."

"I hope so." Feeling insecure, I refused to make eye contact. "Because I love her too. Is that crazy?"

"Not any crazier than you talking to yourself this morning."

I hadn't been talking to myself. How was it my fault that they were too sleepy to notice the nurse walk in? The drugs weren't making me nauseated like they usually did; that had to be a good sign, right?

"I'm gonna go grab some grub. Why don't you shower so that your girlfriend actually wants to lie next to you." Gabe's eyebrows wiggled. "And I'll get you some coffee."

"Good man." I laughed.

Gabe left. I moved to press my call button just as Angela walked back in the room.

"Need help?"

"That I do." I smiled. "I just need to get showered, and I was wondering… would it be possible for me to wear something other than a hospital gown today? I mean, now that the drugs are in my system, I'm just hanging out until surgery, right?"

"Of course." Angela winked. "I think jeans and a white t-shirt are just what the doctor ordered."

I exhaled in relief. "Thanks."

"No problem! Now let's get you ready for that future wife of yours."

"Never going to live that down, am I?" I teased.

"I like it when people speak things into their lives. You want her to be your wife; it will happen. I know it may sound silly, but I admire your faith. Not just in yourself, but in other people. It's commendable, and you need to know — faith doesn't go unnoticed. Just like selflessness — it's always noticed, always rewarded, and should never be taken for granted."

I smiled, though I was a bit confused. Seriously, this nurse was deep. I'd spent a lot of time at hospitals and never met anyone so encouraging. She just made me feel good. Like the path I was taking was the right one. She didn't give me sad eyes, the kind that doctors give you when they know they're going to see you for the last time. Maybe that's why I liked her. Her eyes held hope and amusement as if she knew some giant secret that I was about to find out.

We spent the day in bed. All four of us. It was comical, to say the least. As promised, I was allowed to wear a t-shirt and jeans, which made it easier to hold Kiersten without mooning everyone else. She was sitting between my legs and leaning back against my chest. Every once in a while, I'd feel her hand tap our cadence against my leg as if she was reminding me that we keep our own time. That time was ours.

Halfway through the last episode of Pinky and the Brain that we could find on YouTube, my dad waltzed in, a few people behind him.

What was he doing?

"Thought you kids would be hungry." He grinned and moved out of the way as people began setting up something I can only describe as a buffet fit for a king.

"Is that—" Gabe pointed at a giant Salmon fillet.

"Anthony's catering." Dad nodded proudly. "At your service."

"Best. Food. Ever." Gabe's mouth dropped open again as he greedily watched the food.

The smell was heavenly. Holy crap! I owed my dad big for this.

Small plastic cups were handed to everyone, and my dad pulled out a bottle of chilled champagne. "Now, I'm not one for underage drinking." And he really wasn't. The one time he caught me partying, I'd been grounded for two months. "But, I thought we'd do a toast to my son, Wes."

Kiersten squeezed my leg.

Champagne was poured into every glass. I knew that I would only be able to eat and drink for another hour before I was told to cut it for my surgery, so I snatched the cup.

"May you have happy dreams and wake up refreshed and ready for surgery. To my son, my fighter, my hero." Dad lifted the cup into the air.

"Cheers," everyone said in unison. But I couldn't find my voice. I stared hard at my dad. He was the brave one, not me. He'd watched his wife and son die, and now his only living blood relative was going in for a life-altering surgery. Me? Brave? Nah, the ones that stay behind, the ones that fight alongside you, those are the brave ones. It's easy to go into surgery; you fall asleep. My battle was almost over, I'd tell my body to fight, and then I'd let the doctors do their jobs.

But theirs? I looked around to the faces of my friends and family — their battle was just beginning.

"Thanks, Dad." I lifted my glass to him and took a sip. "For everything."

"Son, I am so damn proud of you."

My dad had never said that to me before, let alone in front of a room full of people. He gave one final nod and walked out the door.

Gabe jumped to his feet and ran out of the room. I knew the guy was fighting his own demons, so I didn't fault him that. He probably just needed a minute alone.

"Should we eat?" Lisa asked, breaking the silence.

"I'm starved." I got up from the bed and started making myself a plate. Gabe returned without saying anything about his quick exit.

The food was incredible. I ate until I couldn't eat anymore.

It was nearing seven. I stopped eating, drank some water, and lay down on the bed, pulling Kiersten into my body so we could spoon.

"Okay, Lisa." Gabe grabbed her hand. "I think that's our cue to exit." He grinned. "See you tomorrow, man." He gave me a fist bump and walked Lisa out of the room.

"Are you scared?" Kiersten asked.

"Are you?"

"I asked you first."

Laughing, I tucked her hair behind her ear and whispered, "I'll just do it afraid."

FORTY-FOUR

For some reason, I wasn't scared... it was weird. An eerie peace descended over that room, and I couldn't explain it.

Kiersten

"**I**'m sorry." Wes kissed my forehead.

I turned to face him. "For what?"

"I told you I'd help you with some of the list." He laughed and shook his head. "Ways to live... Damn, I thought you knew my secret right then and there."

I shrugged. "We all suffer deaths in our lives, right? We all suffer with darkness... mine was just different than yours."

"But not any less serious." Wes touched my cheek. "At any rate, I'm sorry we didn't finish everything."

I pulled away. "Are you talking about the cranberry sauce? Because we had that at Thanksgiving."

"No." He bit down on his lips. "The other stuff."

"Hmm..." I'd been keeping the list in my pocket since he'd been in the hospital. The paper was crumpled and had clearly seen better days. I carefully unfolded it and showed it to Wes. "The list is done."

A line was drawn through every last thing except for what I knew Wes was talking about. "You have a pen?"

He gave me a confused look, then reached to his tray where he'd been playing tic-tac-toe with Gabe and handed me the pen.

Emotion clogged my throat as I carefully drew a line through *Fall in love*, then drew another line through *Get heart broken*. Wes inhaled sharply as my pen hovered over the last line. This time I circled it. *Fall in love anyway*.

A tear rolled down my cheek and landed on the piece of paper.

Wes pulled my face toward his, cupping my cheeks with his hands. "I love you, Kiersten."

"I love you too," I choked out. "So much it hurts. It actually hurts."

He closed his eyes and touched his forehead to mine. "You're going to marry me someday."

"Oh, I am?" I said through my tears.

"Yup." He smiled. "I'm going to get down on one knee, and I'm going to ask you to marry me. I'm not a very patient guy, so I'll let you do two years of school before I pop the question, no more than two years."

"What if I don't want two years?"

His eyes opened.

"What if I want now?"

Wes chuckled lightly. "And have your Uncle Jobob hunt me down? I'd rather not…"

"Fine, one year." My eyes narrowed in a silent challenge.

"One year from this day…" Wes whispered.

I nodded.

"And you'll be saying I do."

"And we'll keep our own time." I closed my eyes and memorized the feel of his face in my hands. "And we'll have three kids."

"Four," he argued. "Always go for an even number."

"And we'll live—"

"Wherever the hell we want."

"But I will need to finish school." I sighed and kissed him on the cheek. "Even though you're loaded, I have to finish school — I chose a major."

"You did?" Wes sat up. "Why didn't you tell me?"

"It was a surprise." I grinned through my tears. "Want to know what it is?"

"Teacher?" he guessed.

"Nope."

"Exotic Dancer?"

I laughed. "Is that a major?"

"It should be."

"Nursing," I whispered. "I want to be a nurse. I want to help in the cancer units. I want — I want to help people like you helped me. I want to help them push away the nightmares, the darkness. I want to rescue them like you rescued me." I felt more tears stream down my face. "You rescued me, and I found my ruin." I bit down on my lip. "I'm ruined for you — and I won't ever be the same. It's the greatest gift anyone's ever given me."

He wiped away my tears. "Ruin?"

"Yeah, a ruin, because in helping me knock down all those demons, you built me back up again. And for that, I'll never be able to repay you."

"Which is why we're having four kids, not three," he whispered.

I laughed and wrapped my arms around his neck. "I love you."

"I love you too… being with you has been the greatest gift anyone could ever give me, and to think it was all because you assaulted me on your first day of class."

"I did not—"

"Shh, Lamb." Wes's lips touched mine. His tongue tasted like champagne. I kissed him back with everything I had inside of me. The kiss wasn't the end. It was the beginning, the beginning of our life together.

We kissed until my mouth was swollen from his lips. He tasted every part of me yet refused to take what I wanted to give him most — myself. He said he wanted something to look forward to when he woke up. Leave it to Wes to use sex as a reason not to die. I had to laugh at his explanation. Then the laughter faded to soft gasps and quiet sighs as his hands roamed all over my body, kissing my chest, my arms, my fingers; he even ran his hands up my calves, kissing the back of my knees as if knees were so special they deserved attention too.

I moaned when his mouth returned to mine and twisted my hands in his dark blond hair. Our tongues danced, our mouths pushed, lips pressed, bodies as close as our clothes would actually allow us. I fell asleep with my mouth on his. He fell asleep with his hands bracing my hips. When I woke up, I was starting the countdown until I married that man. A year from that day. A year from December fifth, and I was going to be Mrs. Kiersten Michels.

FORTY-FIVE

I dreamt of my mom. Of her long blond hair and happy blue eyes. She was so beautiful. She asked me if I was scared. I told her no. We were sitting on the red swing set my dad had bought me for my sixth birthday. She lifted my hands to her lips and kissed my fingers, and told me that it would be okay. For some reason, I believed her. Before she disappeared, she pressed her hands to my chest and closed her eyes.

Weston

"**W**es," Angela murmured. "It's time to get up, sweetie. We've got to get you prepped."

I yawned and nodded, then nudged Kiersten awake. She clung to me for a few brief minutes before leaving the room. I'd see her right before I went in, and I knew she wanted to go get changed since the surgery was going to be at least ten hours.

"How do you feel?" Angela asked like she always did.

"Good." My eyes narrowed. "So strange. I had a dream about my mom. You look a lot like her."

"Really?" She tilted her head. "I imagine she was beautiful, so I'll take that as a compliment."

I laughed as she helped me into the hospital gown. "Oh, she was, believe me."

Once I was in the gown, Angela hooked up my IV again and gave me some anti-nausea medication. It was over really quick. My dad came in to give me a hug. Lisa strolled in with a balloon and a teddy bear.

I took the gift and gave her a hug.

The football team didn't know I was in surgery. My professors didn't know. But Coach did, so when he walked into the room bawling like a baby, it didn't take me by surprise. We'd been through hell and back. It was surreal seeing a three-hundred-pound lineman cry — he'd played for Florida State around twenty years ago. He shook his head and grabbed my hand.

"You beat this, and I'll let you play in the bowl game."

Laughing, I squeezed his hand. "You better let me play. I'm the star quarterback after all."

"That you are." He chuckled and patted my hand. "See you when you wake up."

"When I wake up," I repeated after him as he walked out of my room.

Gabe showed up soon after that.

He sat down in silence.

"You okay, man?" I asked.

"Shouldn't I be asking you that?" He still refused to look at me.

"Gabe…"

"I asked God to give me the cancer. I still wish He would. You're too good, man. You don't… I just—" A string of curses poured out that shocked even me. "My mind still can't comprehend it."

"Stop trying." I sighed. "And remember what I said, let it make you different."

"I've been clean for three years." Gabe rocked back in his chair. "This is the first time since then that I've been tempted to throw it all away. The pain is too much, and then I feel selfish for thinking about myself. I'm not strong like you."

"You are," I argued. "I know you are."

"Thanks." Gabe stood and walked over to me. "Thanks for being my friend."

"Well, Lisa did pay me…" I joked.

"Good to know you still have a sense of humor, jackass." Gabe smacked my shoulder and hugged me so tight I couldn't breathe for a few seconds. "You beat the hell out of this cancer, or I'm hunting you down, got it?"

"Got it."

Gabe started walking out of the room when I called him back. "Gabe?"

"Yeah?"

"Be my best man?"

"Best man?"

"Yeah, in three hundred and sixty-six days, I'm getting married to Kiersten. Be my best man?"

"You've got yourself a deal." He chuckled. "Does Kiersten know about this?"

"Of course. She loves me, you know."

"Yeah, I know." Gabe laughed again. "See you on the other side, man."

Ten minutes went by, and then Kiersten walked in.

She was wearing a white dress.

"Sorry. This was all I could find on short notice."

"You're wearing a—"

"A wedding dress." She laughed. "I thought it would give you some much needed inspiration. Now you can dream about me in a white dress — you taking me out of said white dress — me saying yes when you ask me to marry you… yes to all of the above."

"Come here." I lifted my hands to her. In an instant, she was in my arms, her head buried against my chest. "I love you, Little Lamb."

"I love you too, Wolf." She sobbed. "You're my favorite."

"Favorite what?"

Kiersten drew back, her eyes wide with hope. "Favorite everything. You're my favorite. Out of all the things I could have in the world that would be my favorite, you win. You win all of it."

"Wow, pretty high praise." I smiled and dug my hands into her hair.

"What do you love more?" she teased. "My hair or my heart?"

"Why give me only two choices? Don't leave out your legs, your laugh, the way you bite your lip when you're thinking, the feel of your breath on my face, the sound of your voice in the morning, the way you taste, the three freckles on your nose, the fan of your eyelashes, the caring spirit, the determined soul — so why stop at your hair and your heart? How do you expect me to choose? When what I love the most about you — is you."

I could tell she was trying not to cry. Her face was flushed, her eyes blurred with tears.

"I. Love. You." I looked directly into her eyes. "It's not the end."

"I know," she agreed. "I know it here." She pressed her

hand to my chest, "And I know it here." She moved her hand and pressed it to her own chest. "Have a nice rest, Wes, and know I'll be waiting for you when you wake up."

I nodded.

"It's time." Another nurse walked in, one I didn't recognize. She gave Kiersten a sad smile and escorted her out, just as Angela walked in.

"All right, sweetie." Angela cupped my cheek. "Time to go to sleep, and when you wake up — no more cancer."

Confused, I stared at her, I mean really stared at her, I could have sworn I was looking at my mom. I blinked a few times and shook my head.

"Thank you," I finally said. "You've been a fantastic nurse."

"Remember one thing." She grabbed my bed and began rolling it out the door.

"What?" I asked as she paused in the rolling.

"You may not see every single piece of the puzzle that creates your life — you may not see every move the grand chess player makes — but know, He is in complete control of the game board. Sometimes certain pieces are moved or knocked over to make room for new ones. Other times, things happen because of the world we live in. But everything, in the end, will always turn out for good. It's a nice promise, isn't it? To know that there's a reason for it all? A reason for your cancer — maybe by having cancer, you've saved the lives of three of your best friends. Had you not been sick, would you have met them? Had you not been sick, would you have found the love of your life? Maybe it's not in the perfection of life that things make sense, but in the chaos."

She stood and pushed me down the hall. Her words haunted me the entire way. As I was rolled into the surgical room, I reached for her hand. She gripped mine hard within hers. And then, when I was given the injection to sleep, I looked to my right, at her left hand… on her ring finger was a ring. The exact one my father had given my mom, the one she wore until the day she died. I opened my mouth to say it, but heaviness invaded my eyes; I fell into a deep sleep, a smile on my face.

FORTY-SIX

*Ten hours? What was I supposed to do for ten hours? Pray?
I was praying. I was trying not to cry, and Gabe was trying
to cheer me up by telling me embarrassing stories of Lisa's
childhood — not helpful, but he was trying.*

Kiersten

After five hours, I was ready to go crazy. They said
the surgery could take anywhere from ten to twelve
hours. Randy said that if the doctors came out within
the first hour, it wasn't good news. It meant it was inoperable,
but he had high hopes, so the minute we were out of the woods
after the first two hours had passed, I relaxed a bit.

I looked at the clock again. It was noon. By Five, I should
have Wes back in my arms, hurting, but at least alive. I closed
my eyes and concentrated on his kisses.

Gabe hit me in the arm. I looked up. A doctor was walking
toward us. His head down. *It was too soon. No! No! I knew it
was too soon for him to be briefing us!* My heart faltered and
then thundered against my chest as I gripped Gabe's hand and
waited for the news.

The doctor smiled when Randy stood. Smiling was good

right? I took a deep breath. I would have felt it if Wes's heart stopped beating; I would have known in my soul — he was still with us, he had to be.

"It's the strangest thing..." The doctor shook his head. "The surgery's finished."

"Why is that strange?" Randy asked.

"His tumor." The doctor seemed to be having trouble forming words. "When we looked at it a few days ago, it was the size of the palm of my hand." He held up his hand. "Somehow, over the course of the last few days, it shrunk to the size of a small plum."

"I'm sorry, what?" Randy blinked a few times. I could tell he was trying not to cry.

"The cancer's gone," the doctor said slowly. "It was only in that one location, very near to his heart, but operable. We removed the tumor without any complications. Your son..." The doctor's voice shook, and he drew a tremulous breath. "Your son will live to be a very old man, God willing."

Gabe held me as I collapsed against his chest in thankful sobs.

"When can we see him?" Randy asked, his voice hoarse.

"He's still asleep." The doctor smiled. "I don't know if it was the drugs finally kicking in, or just a miracle. I've worked in the field of oncologic thoracic surgery for fifteen years and never seen anything like it. We'll be examining all the drugs your son took to see if there's something to the combination that shrinks tumors in their final stages."

"All right." Randy held out his hand, and the doctor shook it. "Thank you, thank you for everything."

"It was my pleasure." The doctor nodded to us and walked off.

I couldn't see through my tears.

Gabe's body shook against mine. I thought he was crying, and then I looked up. He was laughing so hard I thought he was going to pass out.

"What's wrong with you?" I pushed against him.

"That bastard made me promise to be his best man." Gabe laughed even louder. "He would live—" Gabe wiped his eyes. "—just to see me in a tux."

I joined in the laughter. Lisa rose from her chair and grabbed my hand in hers. Relief, that's all I felt, relief that he was going to be okay, that we were going to be together. I had to keep myself from running into that operating room and throwing my body against his.

He was alive.

The love of my life was waiting for me.

Holy crap. I was getting married in a year.

Now it was my turn to laugh.

FORTY-SEVEN

I dreamt of Kiersten in a wedding dress. I was at the end of the aisle, and she was walking toward me. Then my brain fast-forwarded to us holding hands and watching our kids play in the yard. And then, even further, I watched our wrinkled hands touch as we were witness to another great-grandchild being brought into the world. My life — my future. It was all her.

Weston

The first thing I saw when I woke up was my dad. He was hovering over my bed with a look of pure awe on his face. The minute I'd seen my mom's wedding ring on Angela's finger, I'd known I was going to be okay. I knew with certainty that I really was just going to take a nap and then wake up and start my life — a new beginning.

Dad's face faded in and out as well as Kiersten's. I had no idea how long I slept. One day, my eyes stayed open. I tried focusing on something — anything. Finally, I was able to see another face. My dad's smile made my chest hurt, either that or my chest just hurt from the surgery; I couldn't tell if it was physical or emotional — nor did I care. It hurt — pain meant that I was living.

"How do you feel?" my dad asked.

"Like a quarterback." My voice was still hoarse from having the tube thrust down it, but I didn't care. I wanted to talk. Talking meant I wasn't dreaming everything up. Every damn breath hurt like hell, but I kept breathing too. I told myself it would be a privilege to breathe through pain like that for the rest of my life — just knowing each breath was a gift.

Dad laughed. "Good, you think Coach will let you play in that bowl game?"

"*When* we get that bowl game," I corrected as I tried to clear my throat and get my voice to sound more normal. "Coach promised me he'd let me play." I winked. "Where is everyone?"

"I wanted a moment..." Dad cleared his throat. "Just to talk to my son. Alone. To make sure it was real. That you were really here and not still in that operating room. Did the doctors tell you what they discovered?"

I nodded. "The tumor shrank."

"Son, the tumor shrank to a quarter of its size, all within four days."

I couldn't trust myself to speak. One nurse called it a miracle while the doctor gave all the credit to the medicine. I guess I'd never know, and maybe it didn't matter how I was spared, just that I was.

"Incredible, right?" I said.

"A miracle." Dad patted my hand, "I love you, Wes."

"Love you too, Dad."

He got up, then paused in the doorway. "You really getting married in a year?"

"Yup." I couldn't hold back my grin; I could have sworn my heart skipped a beat.

He shook his head and laughed. "All right then, guess I

better get to know that girl's family."

Seconds later, Kiersten came rushing into the room. She was like a hot blur of red as she bounced onto my bed, careful not to touch my chest; I mean, I did just have major surgery. She pressed her lips against my mouth and kissed me for a few minutes before pulling back.

"Way ta fight, Wes."

"Some things…" I tucked her red hair behind her ear, "… are worth fighting for."

A nurse walked in and checked my clipboard.

"Where's Angela?" I asked.

The nurse gave me a weird look. "Angela?"

"Yeah, the other nurse that was helping me. She had blond hair, pretty face…"

"Hmm." The nurse put down her clipboard and smiled. "We don't have a nurse named Angela who works anywhere in this unit, at least that I know of. By the looks of your chart, you were on some pretty heavy medication. Hallucinations are completely normal when you have that amount of drugs in your system, Weston. I'll be sure to notify the doctor of the side effects so he can take note of them." She gave me a kind smile and walked out of the room.

"Angela? Who is that?" Kiersten asked.

"I don't think I hallucinated anything. I mean, I did tell you I was going to marry you, right?"

She nodded.

"And you promised to wear a wedding dress?"

Another nod.

"And nakedness, I could have sworn there was nakedness."

Kiersten rolled her eyes. "Yes, lots of nakedness."

"But you don't remember Angela either?" I asked.

"Not at all." She shrugged. "Maybe it was your imagination, or maybe you just had a guardian angel."

We kissed and then heard a knock on the door. A male nurse brought in a tray of food; behind him, I saw a familiar smile, followed by blond hair.

"Is that her?" Kiersten pointed.

Angela gave us a small wave, walked away from the room, and got right on the elevator. Just as the door began to close, she winked at me.

"Holy shit."

Kiersten tapped me on the shoulder. "Who was that?"

I sighed and silently thanked God for miracles of all sizes. "Let me tell you about my mom."

FORTY-EIGHT

Weston

Two months later

Shit, I was nervous as hell. The doctor had said I could play in limited capacity, but he didn't think I'd be able to last a whole game. I mean, who plays after having their chest cracked open? Yet, I felt healthy as a horse. I'd started working out two weeks after my surgery, slowly and surely, I felt healthy again. No more nausea, no more anything. I was alive, and God was I thankful.

Though I was still only allowed to warm the bench and pace back and forth while my team kicked ass.

I waved at Kiersten. She was sitting in the stands with her aunt and uncle. My dad and Jobob had gotten crazy close over the last few months. Crazy, but it seemed that grief on both Kiersten's and my sides brought the men close to one another. It only took about a week for Jobob to get over his star-struck attitude. Within two weeks, he was pulling pranks on my dad that had all of us in stitches. It was good to laugh. It was even better to see my dad laugh.

Dad waved from the sidelines too and pointed at Gabe, who was sitting next to Lisa with a giant sign that read, *Go Wes!* In Red letters. They drew a giant heart around it.

News of my surgery and cancer struggle got out as we all assumed it would. After numerous Skype interviews with Good Morning America and Anderson Cooper, not to mention ESPN, I'd barely had any time to even think about the championship game and about what I was going to do during halftime.

We were playing Oregon. Again. Of all the luck in the world. The Ducks were good, but we were better. I threw the football again and stretched my arms above my head. It was the BCS championship. I should have been thinking about the plays, about not getting hit, about winning — but all I could think about was *her*.

"Ready for this?" Tony asked, throwing the ball one last time.

"Of course." I laughed. "Are you?"

"We're having duck for dinner." He pointed two fingers at me and then threw his head back and howled. People in the stands were shouting green and yellow. I knew Gabe would be pissed. Poor guy, nobody hated the Ducks more than him, though he wouldn't tell any of us the exact reason.

The announcer came on the loudspeaker. Funny, how last time I was on the field, I'd thought my life might be over.

And honestly — it had just begun.

The first two quarters went by in a blur. The score was tied, and I was officially exhausted, just watching. I tried to get coach to put me in a few times, but I was completely ignored;

I felt like I was letting my team down, my fingers itched to touch the pigskin.

"You sure you're up for this?" Dad asked once the buzzer for halftime went off.

"Yup." I licked my lips. "I've been waiting all my life for this."

He dug into his pocket and handed me the box. "Go get 'em."

"If everyone could have a seat, we have a special announcement." The man called over the loudspeaker. I walked to the middle of the field amidst shouts and cheers from all over the stands; even the Duck fans were on their feet.

The minute I turned, I realized why. Every single person on my side of the crowd were flashing shirts that said *I heart Wes Michels*. I was too shocked to say anything. The yells grew louder. I gave a bow and took off my helmet. Nervous, I cleared my throat before speaking into the microphone.

"Thank you," I said in a hoarse voice. "You have no idea how much your support means to me, my family, my team." I cleared my throat again. "I love you guys. All of you, but there's someone... someone special that I really need to talk to right now. Kiersten?" The crowd cheered louder. "Kiersten, can you come down here?"

Amidst screams and hollers, my girl made her way from the stands and across the fields.

"Damn," I said into the microphone. "You're just as beautiful as the first day I saw you."

Her red hair matched her face as she made the final few steps to the middle of the field.

"Lamb," I began. She rolled her eyes, but I could tell she was happy. I fought against the nerves and excitement I felt at finally being able to claim her as my own. "My heart was literally breaking when I met you." The crowd fell silent. "It was getting slowly poisoned by something beyond my control — some think it is a miracle that I'm standing here, others say it was the drugs." I gripped her hands. "But I know the truth."

Kiersten's brow furrowed.

"When I met you — somehow, you healed me. From the inside out, the outside in. We conquered fears together, we learned, we laughed, and we loved. I swear you caused my heart to soar more in the past few months than it has in my entire existence. My heart is whole because you chose to share yours with me, and it's for that reason that I get down on not one, but both knees…" I knelt in front of her and gripped her hand. "And say thank you. Thank you for saving my life, thank you for loving me enough to treasure your own, and thank you for being my strength when I had none. I'd like to think our hearts are joined — forever entwined — but considering that's not technically a legal joining, I have a question for you."

Gasps were heard throughout the stadium.

"Marry me? Make me the happiest man alive." I opened the box, revealing my mom's ring. The same one I saw when I'd closed my eyes before my surgery. It was a three-carat antique-cut diamond solitaire, with the words *My heart for yours* engraved on the inside. Dad said when he engraved it, he had only thought of his love for Mom. Never once did he suspect that it would have a deeper meaning for all of us.

Maybe, just maybe, everything did happen for a reason. Maybe there was no such thing as a coincidence. I gulped, waiting for Kiersten's answer.

With a shout, she threw her arms around my neck, knocking me to my back. Her mouth found mine.

I tasted her lips and growled against them. "That a yes?"

"That's a *what the heck took you so long*?" She smacked me on the chest and then looked away as tears streamed down her face. "I love you Wes Michels."

"Oh, yeah?"

She grinned and pointed to her shirt. "You like?"

"I love."

"I heart Wes Michels," she whispered and kissed my mouth again. "I would have given you mine, you know…"

"What?" I asked confused, still holding her.

"My heart…" Her lower lip trembled. "I would have given it to you — to save you. I would have done anything."

"I'll still take it."

"What?"

"Your heart," I whispered. "I'll still take it, if the offer stands. I want all of it, even the broken pieces, the shredded ones that no longer fit. I want all of them — all of you. I need it all."

"You have it." She tightened her grip around my neck as she jumped into my arms and wrapped her legs around my waist.

Camera crews were going crazy, trying to get every angle of our bodies, and then, exactly as I'd planned it, the fireworks went off in perfect tune with the song *Beneath Your Beautiful*.

"Wow." She breathed, letting her head fall back as she looked at the sky. "You do things big, don't you?"

"I am a Michels." I winked. "Now, let's go win that game."

We could have lost, and I would have still been happy. Luckily, we didn't. The green and yellow were no more. Gabe looked ready to cry tears of joy, and then he started trash-talking, so we escorted him away from other fans.

I grabbed Kiersten's hand and kissed it.

I just wanted to get her home.

Being named MVP? Meant nothing. NFL scouts? Nothing. But Kiersten? Hell, yeah. She was everything. I left early. I said goodbye to the cameras, the lights, the fame — I just wanted her. And in that dark tunnel, as we walked out of the stadium, feeling my mom's ring against her finger, I knew I was starting the rest of my life.

WANT MORE RUIN?

I hope you enjoyed Ruin!
If you want to read Gabe or Lisa's story,
here is the reading order!

Ruin (Wes Michels & Kiersten's story)
Toxic (Gabe Hyde & Saylor's story)
Fearless (Wes Michels & Kiersten's story)
Shame (Tristan & Lisa's story)

WANT MORE YA ROMANCE?

If you enjoyed this book, then you will also love these Young Adult Romances:

Ruin Series
Ruin (Wes Michels & Kiersten's story)
Toxic (Gabe Hyde & Saylor's story)
Fearless (Wes Michels & Kiersten's story)
Shame (Tristan & Lisa's story)

Seaside Series
Tear (Alec, Demetri & Natalee's story)
Pull (Demetri & Alyssa's story)
Shatter (Alec & Natalee's story)
Forever (Alec & Natalee's story)
Fall (Jamie Jaymeson & Pricilla's story)
Strung (Tear + from the boys POV)
Eternal (Demetri & Alyssa's story)

Other Titles
Every Girl Does It (Preston & Amanda's story)
Compromising Kessen (Christian & Kessen's story)

ORIGINAL DEDICATION FROM 2012

Uncle JoBob, when I think of you, when I hear your name, the word that comes to mind is *brave*. The next word? *Hero*. The next one after that? *Peace*. You are walking peace, you are a fighter, and you are a walking example of what I hope to be in my everyday life. I admire your courage so much. You don't let cancer get you down; rather than allowing it to get you down, you use it as a way to lift others up. Words can't express the impact you have made on my life.

To my dear mother-in-law who fought breast cancer, stared it in the face and didn't back down — I love you.

To Monica — girl, you've got this. You're going to beat this, and then you're going to have a glass of wine and read a book.

To everyone who's lost someone to cancer, to anyone fighting the war against it — to the doctors, to the families, to the loved ones who buried their soul mates.

My heart is with you.
This book —
This is for you.

ABOUT THE AUTHOR

Rachel Van Dyken is the #1 *New York Times*, *Wall Street Journal*, and *USA Today* bestselling author of over 90 books ranging from contemporary romance to paranormal. With over four million copies sold, she's been featured in *Forbes*, *US Weekly*, and *USA Today*. Her books have been translated in more than 15 countries. She was one of the first romance authors to have a Kindle in Motion book through Amazon publishing and continues to strive to be on the cutting edge of the reader experience. She keeps her home in the Pacific Northwest with her husband, adorable sons, naked cat, and two dogs. For more information about her books and upcoming events, visit www.RachelVanDykenauthor.com.

ALSO BY RACHEL VAN DYKEN

Kathy Ireland & Rachel Van Dyken
Fashion Jungle

Rachel Van Dyken & M. Robinson
Mafia Casanova (Romeo & Eden's story)
Falling for the Villain (Juliet Sinacore's story)

Eagle Elite
Elite (Nixon & Trace's story)
Elect (Nixon & Trace's story)
Entice (Chase & Mil's story)
Elicit (Tex & Mo's story)
Bang Bang (Axel & Amy's story)
Enforce (Elite + from the boys POV)
Ember (Phoenix & Bee's story)
Elude (Sergio & Andi's story)
Empire (Sergio & Val's story)
Enrage (Dante & El's story)
Eulogy (Chase & Luciana's story)
Exposed (Dom & Tanit's story)
Envy (Vic & Renee's story)

Elite Bratva Brotherhood
RIP (Nikolai & Maya's story)
Debase (Andrei & Alice's story)

Mafia Royals Romances
Royal Bully (Asher & Claire's story)
Ruthless Princess (Serena & Junior's story)
Scandalous Prince (Breaker & Violet)
Destructive King (Asher & Annie)
Mafia King (TBA)
Fallen Dynasty (TBA)

Covet
Stealing Her (Bridge & Isobel's story)
Finding Him (Julian & Keaton's story)

The Dark Ones Series
The Dark Ones (Ethan & Genesis's story)
Untouchable Darkness (Cassius & Stephanie's story)
Dark Surrender (Alex & Hope's story)
Darkest Temptation (Mason & Serenity's story)
Darkest Sinner (Timber & Kyra's story)

Wingmen Inc.
The Matchmaker's Playbook (Ian & Blake's story)
The Matchmaker's Replacement (Lex & Gabi's story)

Bro Code
Co-Ed (Knox & Shawn's story)
Seducing Mrs. Robinson (Leo & Kora's story)
Avoiding Temptation (Slater & Tatum's story)
The Setup (Finn & Jillian's story)

Liars, Inc
Dirty Exes (Colin, Jessie & Blaire's story)
Dangerous Exes (Jessie & Isla's story)

Cruel Summer Trilogy
Summer Heat (Marlon & Ray's story)
Summer Seduction (Marlon & Ray's story)
Summer Nights (Marlon & Ray's story)

Curious Liaisons
Cheater (Lucas & Avery's story)
Cheater's Regret (Thatch & Austin's story)

Red Card
Risky Play (Slade & Mackenzie's story)
Kickin' It (Matt & Parker's story)

Players Game
Fraternize (Miller, Grant and Emerson's story)
Infraction (Miller & Kinsey's story)
M.V.P. (Jax & Harley's story)

The Consequence Series
The Consequence of Loving Colton (Colton & Milo's story)
The Consequence of Revenge (Max & Becca's story)
The Consequence of Seduction (Reid & Jordan's story)
The Consequence of Rejection (Jason & Maddy's story)

The Bet Series
The Bet (Travis & Kacey's story)
The Wager (Jake & Char Lynn's story)
The Dare (Jace & Beth Lynn's story)

The Bachelors of Arizona
The Bachelor Auction (Brock & Jane's story)
The Playboy Bachelor (Bentley & Margot's story)
The Bachelor Contract (Brant & Nikki's story)

Ruin Series
Ruin (Wes Michels & Kiersten's story)
Toxic (Gabe Hyde & Saylor's story)
Fearless (Wes Michels & Kiersten's story)
Shame (Tristan & Lisa's story)

Seaside Series
Tear (Alec, Demetri & Natalee's story)
Pull (Demetri & Alyssa's story)
Shatter (Alec & Natalee's story)
Forever (Alec & Natalee's story)
Fall (Jamie Jaymeson & Pricilla's story)
Strung (Tear + from the boys POV)
Eternal (Demetri & Alyssa's story)

Seaside Pictures
Capture (Lincoln & Dani's story)
Keep (Zane & Fallon's story)
Steal (Will & Angelica's story)
All Stars Fall (Trevor & Penelope's story)
Abandon (Ty & Abigail's story)
Provoke (Braden & Piper's story)
Surrender (Andrew & Bronte's story)

Single Titles
A Crown for Christmas (Fitz & Phillipa's story)
Every Girl Does It (Preston & Amanda's story)
Compromising Kessen (Christian & Kessen's story)
Divine Uprising (Athena & Adonis's story)
The Parting Gift — written with Leah Sanders (Blaine and Mara's story)

Waltzing With The Wallflower — written with Leah Sanders
Waltzing with the Wallflower (Ambrose & Cordelia)
Beguiling Bridget (Anthony & Bridget's story)
Taming Wilde (Colin & Gemma's story)

London Fairy Tales
Upon a Midnight Dream (Stefan & Rosalind's story)
Whispered Music (Dominique & Isabelle's story)
The Wolf's Pursuit (Hunter & Gwendolyn's story)
When Ash Falls (Ashton & Sofia's story)

Renwick House
The Ugly Duckling Debutante (Nicholas & Sara's story)
The Seduction of Sebastian St. James (Sebastian & Emma's story)
The Redemption of Lord Rawlings (Phillip & Abigail's story)
An Unlikely Alliance (Royce & Evelyn's story)
The Devil Duke Takes a Bride (Benedict & Katherine's story)

RACHEL VAN DYKEN
www.rachelvandykenauthor.com

Made in the USA
Las Vegas, NV
23 January 2021